The Tale of Irwyn Tremayne

Frances Hern

◆ FriesenPress

Suite 300 - 990 Fort St
Victoria, BC, V8V 3K2
Canada

www.friesenpress.com

ISBN
978-1-4602-9047-7 (Hardcover)
978-1-4602-9048-4 (Paperback)
978-1-4602-9049-1 (eBook)

1. FICTION

Distributed to the trade by The Ingram Book Company

To read *The Tale of Irwyn Tremayne* is to delight in the adventure of perilous sea passage. Frances Hern writes with a flair for palpable detail and possibility. The result is a hair-raising account that will capture any young reader's imagination. Young Irwyn Tremayne escapes his own secret and fear headfirst into a world of thievery, sailor's knots, scurvy, opium, distant lands and even love.

Lisa Murphy-Lamb, author of *Dinosaur Hunters* and *Jesus on The Dashboard*

For Claire, Adrienne and Ian, who introduced me to a new generation of books and reminded me what it is like to be fifteen.

Prologue

In the nineteenth century, miners from Cornwall and West Devon, in the south of England, travelled to many countries including Spain, Cuba, North and South America, Australia and South Africa. They were nicknamed Cousin Jacks because they stuck together and worked hard to promote themselves as the best metal miners in the world. Some of them may have left England for the adventure. Others probably hoped for a better life. Up until the end of the nineteenth century, education in Britain was generally available only to those who could afford to pay for it so most of these men had no formal education. Their only knowledge of their journey, and the countries they were travelling to, came from what they had heard by word of mouth.

While the characters in this book, and their circumstances, are entirely fictional, around the year 1838, a group of 37 miners left St. Austell in Cornwall to re-work an old Spanish copper mine on Virgin Gorda, one of the British Virgin Islands.

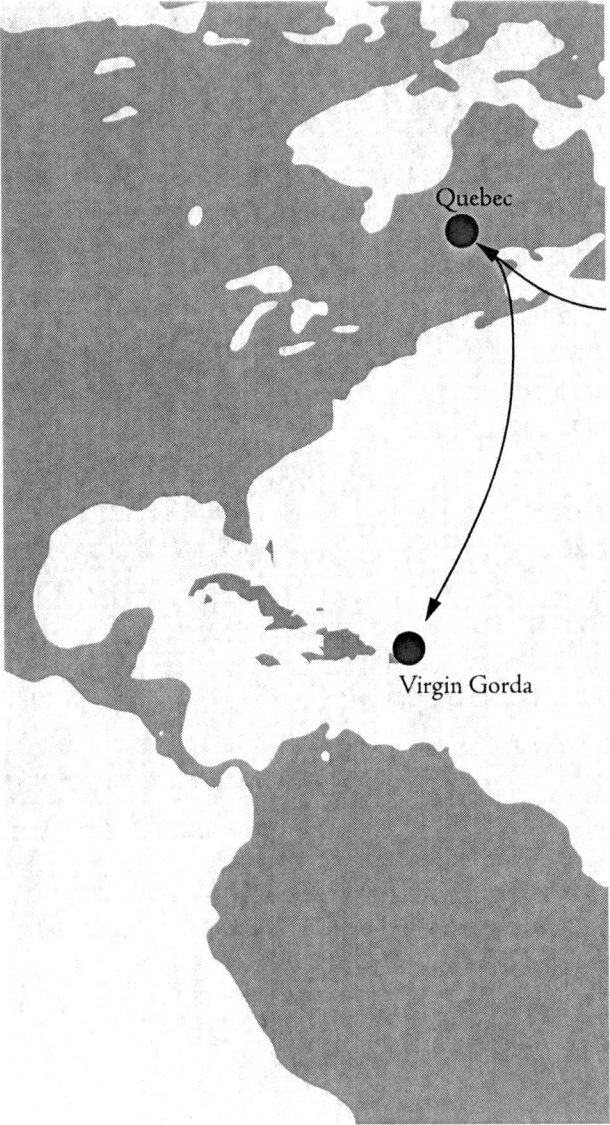

Quebec

Virgin Gorda

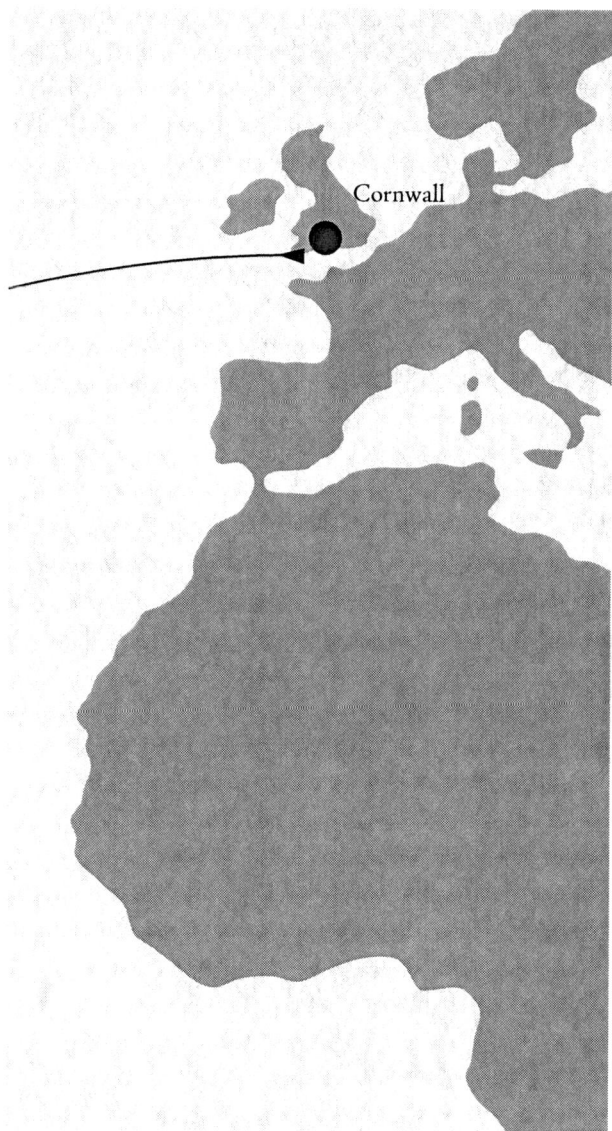

Cornwall

Part One
The Copper Mine

Chapter 1

"Irwyn Tremayne, I need another barrow boy!"

My heart took off like a spooked horse as the mine captain bellowed my name from the shed doorway. I saw myself wheeling barrows of blasted ore through black, suffocating tunnels as rock seams crumbled and boulders blocked my way out. I couldn't breathe. I wanted to say yes, sir. Wanted to please the captain. Father too. But my head screamed NO and the words fought in my throat.

"Come on." He stepped into the shed. "I've got younger boys wanting to take your place here."

Muscles twitched along his jaw line as the seconds stretched out. I tried to swallow what felt like a mouthful of tailings. Then Jimmy, who was working next to me, stepped forward.

"I'll be yer barrow boy, sir."

The captain looked him over. Jimmy was twelve, two years younger than me but a good two hands taller and of sturdy build. His trousers were mostly flour-sack patches held up with a piece of old rope. He'd earn extra wages working below ground.

"Come along then, boy."

Jimmy grinned at me before following the captain across the yard. When they were out of earshot, the jeers began.

"Irwyn the earywig," sang one of the other boys. "You'll have to scuttle faster than that if you want to get on."

I ignored the sniggers, grabbed my sieve with shaking hands and plunged it into the tank. The copper ore inside shifted as water swirled through it. Heavier chunks of ore rattled to the bottom. Lighter pieces floated to the surface. The captain would be back tomorrow, or next week, wanting to put me to work below ground. If I didn't look like the runt of the litter, he'd have done so long ago.

If only I'd left with Uncle Glen after Mother's funeral. I don't know why I thought I'd be able to change Father's mind about me working in Uncle's inn in Truro.

"Tremaynes are miners," Father'd argued, when I told him I didn't want to work in the mine. "You don't want to go traipsing around the country when you can earn a good wage here. Besides, you can't think only of yourself. One day you'll have a family relying on you."

But I woke drenched in sweat from dreams of working underground. And how could I leave Father now?

An almighty crack of thunder startled me so I dropped my sieve into the tank. Icy water drenched me and I spat out its metallic taste. Clouds had turned the sky the colour of mouldy mushrooms. Lightning zigzagged beyond the mine's headgear, the tall wooden frame with pulleys for hoisting ore to the surface. Thunder rolled again and again. It boomed and shook our shed like the captain in one of his rages. One of the younger boys began to cry. The rest of us crowded around the doorway and watched. Fat raindrops gathered speed until they formed a grey wall that hid the other buildings. The yard turned to mire as pellets pounded the ground. I'd never seen rain like this.

After a while the thunder and lightning passed over but the rain kept on. The other boys went back to jigging. There was so much rain, the mine's pumps worked full time to drain the lower levels. They'd be filling up with all this extra water pouring in and the long ladders back to the surface would be wet and slippery. Henry, my older brother, was nimble and alert, but what about Father?

"Please let Mr. Gribble be with him," I prayed.

Shouts sounded over the clank of chains that hauled buckets of ore to the surface, and the din of the stamps that pounded and crushed the ore. I slopped across the yard jumping over puddles. My optimistic mother had bought my boots with growing room. As one stuck in the mud, my bare foot slid out and squelched into the mire. I thrust it back into my boot and knotted the broken lace. Rain battered my back. So much for keeping dry.

Mrs. Gribble, a neighbour, was huddled under the overhang of the count house roof with other women who should have been breaking up the ore. I squeezed in beside her.

"Where's Henry blasting?" she asked.

"The hundred fathom lead to the east," I said.

"He'll be above flood level then. And don't you worry about your father," she added, as though she could read my mind. "Jago will be with him."

Jago Gribble had teamed up with Father before I was born. They had a knack for knowing how much ore a pitch held and how much they should bid to work on it. They did well together. Or had, until Mother died, eighteen days before Christmas, and the strange moods came over Father. Mr. Gribble looked out for him but the mine was a dangerous place for anyone without his wits about him.

I sloshed over to the pithead doorway and peered in to see what was happening. The captain was too busy shouting orders to notice me creep inside and lean into a shadowy corner. Two men had roped themselves to the shaft entrance where they could help haul out exhausted workers. Another man was digging a trench to divert a stream of water running in beneath the doorway and down the main shaft. Two girls were piling earth into a barrier in front of the shaft. I grabbed a spade and ran to help. The gush of water gradually eased but how many more places had rainwater running into the mine?

Someone shouted, "That's it. Steady now," as the first bedraggled miner was helped from the top of the shaft. More miners appeared. One pulled a colleague up the last rungs of the ladder. I didn't need to see the face beneath its streaks of dirt to recognize the rescuer.

"Henry!"

I almost flung my arms around him but thought better of it. Henry ruffled my hair and grinned.

"All right, Wyn?" he asked.

"Father and Mr. Gribble are still in the mine."

"They were deeper," Henry said. "It'll take them longer to get out." But his grin had gone.

The trickle of tired, wet miners continued, their names called out to the accountant who checked them against a long list of men still below ground.

"Charles Tremelling."

"Sam and Pete Penberthy."

The men went off to change out of wet work clothes. Even so, the room around the main shaft grew more crowded as newcomers pressed in hoping to find husbands, sons, and brothers. Wet woolen clothes and smoke from a couple of the men's pipes hid the horrible earthy smell of the mine. My chilblained hands began to burn and I felt warm for the first time since I'd left my bed that morning. I leaned against a wooden post, closed my eyes and willed Father and Mr. Gribble up to the surface.

* * *

"Wyn."

I jumped as Henry shook my arm. My throat tightened. I glanced towards the shaft.

"Father?" I croaked.

"No," said Henry. "But there's a lull. Let's go and look for him."

"You want *me* to search the mine with you?"

"This is your chance to come down with me and get you used to it. It's not as bad as you imagine. You'll see."

People were looking at us. I could just imagine the gossip if I refused. It spread through Redruth faster than measles. Henry hung a coil of rope across one shoulder, grabbed a spare hat and slapped it on my head. It was too big but would have to do. He lit another candle from his own and stuck it in the crown of my hat with a lump of clay.

"Just follow me," he said as I hesitated. "You can do it."

Now Mrs. Gribble was watching us. I pictured Father wandering through dark tunnels as they filled with water. My mouth was too dry to speak so I nodded to Henry who yelled into the shaft.

"Anyone below?"

I'd have given my soul to hear Father's voice call up but there was only silence.

"Coming down," Henry yelled. He began to climb down the ladder. I gripped the sides and stepped onto the first rung. I could do this.

My knees shook. I stopped a few rungs down and peered into the mine's dark throat. Shadows flickered around me as my hat wobbled and I quickly straightened up again. The mine couldn't really swallow me up.

"All right?" Henry called, from somewhere below.

I took a deep breath then squeaked out "Yes."

I stepped onto the next rung and began to count aloud, trying to banish the scary pictures that flashed though my head. When I reached nineteen, I couldn't remember what came next. I began again at number one.

We were on our fourth ladder when I heard voices.

"A great gush of water doused our candles," said someone below me. "We had to feel our way to the ladders."

"I've never prayed so hard in my life," said someone else.

Twelve more rungs and I reached the small landing where Henry was waiting for me. Two miners were making their way to the surface. One pulled a spare candle from his pocket and held it against Henry's to light it.

"Have you seen my father, Thomas Tremayne?" I asked.

"He weren't working anywhere near us," said the one with the candle. Then they both squeezed around me and climbed on up. It was all I could do not to follow them.

"All right, Wyn?" Henry asked.

"No. I hate this." It came out louder than I intended.

"You'll get used to it. You're doing really well. Come on."

He started down the next ladder. How many ladders were there? Perhaps I was better not knowing. The two miners disappeared into the gloom above me. Water dripped from slimy walls that looked like the sides of a huge grave. I shivered. But I could do this. I *was* doing it and perhaps Father would be pleased and snap out of his black moods. I risked another glance down. Henry was way below me again. My brain flashed a picture of Father thrashing around as he tried to hold his head above water. I hurried after Henry. That's when everything went wrong.

Chapter 2

I was trying to catch up to Henry when my foot, still slimy with mud, skidded inside my wet boot. I cried out and clutched the ladder as my feet shot out from under me and my hat slid from my head. For a moment shadows flickered and swirled. There was another cry and everything went dark. My feet dangled above the gaping maw of the mine.

My heart was thumping its way out of my chest. I groped for the ladder with my feet. Found a rung to rest them on. I'd seen mangled bodies of miners who blacked out and fell while climbing to the surface at the end of their shift. Splintered bones sticking through flesh. Skulls smashed like pumpkins. The ladder seemed to sway. I gripped harder. Closed my eyes. Thought, I am not going to die. I am not going to die.

* * *

I don't know how long I leaned against that ladder hanging on to those six words. I became aware of water dripping, the lifeless smell of the mine. When I could breathe properly, I called out.

"Henry? HENNNREEE."

Did someone answer way below or was it an echo? I opened my eyes but couldn't see a thing. I forced the fingers of my right hand to uncurl, let go of the rung, and moving only one hand or one foot at a time I crawled back up the ladder to the platform above, where I sat hugging my knees to my chest. There was no light below me. Why couldn't I see Henry's candle? Was he all right? I was cold but sweat beaded my forehead. I knew only one thing. I couldn't go down.

"It would be stupid," I said aloud, for the comfort of hearing my voice. "I don't know where I'm going. I can't see anything. I'll get lost and be one more person to be rescued." Or worse.

Something skittered past. I prayed it was a rat and not one of the knockers who lived in the mine and grew mean if they weren't treated right. I stifled a sob and tried to think.

If I waited maybe Henry'd come back to see what had happened to me. But what if he didn't? What if *he* needed help? I stretched out stiff arms and legs. A deep breath came out as a sob. If Henry wasn't all right I was abandoning him. But what could I do if I went on down? I felt for the ladder and began to climb.

Black void gradually gave way to grey gloom. The men roped to the shaft entrance had gone. I crawled out onto the surface. There was no sign of Mrs. Gribble or the captain. I walked up to someone who was organizing rescuers into groups.

"My brother…" My voice cracked. I cleared my throat as the man turned towards me and tried again. "Henry's down there looking for Father." I pointed towards the shaft. "They might need help."

"All right, sonny," said the man. "We'll see what we can find."

I prayed Henry had gone on down without me. That I hadn't seen his light because he was too far away. I couldn't think about the alternative. But had that second cry come from me or from Henry?

I had to escape the mine's dank smell of death. Outside, the steam engines that pulled buckets of ore to the surface were still running. A row of miners appeared clinging to the bucket chains like a string of onions. They dropped to the ground one by one and I stared at the last two onions. Father! And Mr. Gribble.

I realized it had stopped raining as I rushed over to where they dripped and shook in the cold February afternoon. Father grabbed Mr. Gribble's hand with both of his.

"If you hadn't held my hands around that chain, I'd still be down there," he said, uttering more words than he'd said since Mother died.

"You'd have done the same for me." Mr. Gribble sounded as though there was something stuck in his throat. When they loosed hands, he bent to roll up a trouser leg. His knee was swollen like a giant beetroot.

"Oh my," said Mrs. Gribble, trotting up as Father caught sight of me. "We'll bind that up and get you home."

"Where's Henry?" asked Father

"Down the mine," I said.

"But he was with you," said Mrs. Gribble.

"No," I cried. "Well, yes, he was."

My voice was too loud. People stared at us. I should have told Father then what had really happened but other people were listening.

"We… we went to look for you in the mine, Father, but Henry was way ahead of me and my candle went out and I couldn't see. I called to Henry but he didn't answer. So I came back up."

"And Henry's still in the mine," said Father.

I nodded, wondering whether my burning cheeks looked as red as they felt. But that *was* the truth. Some of it.

"Go home," said Father. His mouth made a tight line.

"What are you going to do?"

"Find Henry."

And they'd both be safe by now but for me.

"But you're cold and wet."

And what if the strangeness came over him again?

"Go home Wyn."

With that, he turned and strode towards the mine office.

"He'll find Henry," said Mrs. Gribble. "Help me take Jago home."

"You can't let him go back down the mine," I cried. "Not on his own."

"He's got more sense than to go on his own," said Mr. Gribble. "Besides, I can barely walk with this knee, let alone climb ladders."

"Give Mr. Gribble an arm," said Mrs. Gribble.

I shook my head. "I'm waiting for Father."

"Then don't go upsetting yourself," said Mrs. Gribble. "Henry knows the mine. He'll be all right. You'll see."

I stared after the Gribbles and tried to push pictures of what I might see out of my mind. What if it *was* one of the knockers who'd run past me in the mine? I should have asked for help instead of acting like a baby. I turned and followed Father to the office. Standing outside the open door, I could hear the captain's voice.

"We've forty-three men missing," he said. "Two search gangs have already started down. You can join the third."

It was growing dark and I stepped back into the shadows as Father came out of the office with three other men. I wanted to shout that he shouldn't go, that he was exhausted, but my mind kept replaying the second cry as the candle on

my falling hat went out. A cold, heavy stone settled in the pit
of my stomach.

Chapter 3

"Pull … pull … pull," called one of the miners. We heaved ropes over pulleys to haul the first casualty to the surface. In the gloom I glimpsed his shape and my heart flipped. It wasn't Henry. The boy screamed as they lowered him onto a litter. His right leg stuck out at an impossible angle and water dripped red from his trousers. Trousers held together with flour-sack patches. Jimmy!

My knees felt funny and I leaned against a post. Jimmy thought he'd pulled a fast one by taking my job of barrow boy. Would he now lose his leg? Dr. Basset helped carry the litter away to the warmth of the engine room. I tried to stop shaking. Maybe I was hungry. It was hours since lunchtime and my pasty was still in the jigging shed, if no one had eaten it. I was about to go and see when someone helped Father out of the mine shaft. I knew he shouldn't have gone down again. His face had that awful vacant look that came with his strange moods. I dragged a wooden crate over for him to sit on and a woman handed him a mug of tea. He wrapped his hands around the steaming mug and stared at nothing.

"Father?"

He didn't respond. The men on the ropes hauled another casualty to the surface. I prayed Henry would be found so I could take Father home and someone must have heard me because next thing I knew they were hauling another miner out of the shaft and it *was* Henry and he seemed fine. Not screaming or moaning or dripping blood. No misshapen limbs. Then they swung him around.

His eyes were closed. His head flopped as they laid him onto a push cart. I walked towards him. Everyone grew still and quiet.

The man who'd helped Father out of the shaft looked at me and shook his head. Such a small movement. Did I imagine it? Whining filled my ears. I moved through mud, every step an effort.

"Henry?" I crept forward. In the flickering candlelight he looked as though he was asleep. I squeezed his cold hand. He didn't squeeze back.

"His hand was sticking out of the water," said the man, "his arm wedged above his head between two rocks."

Henry's nails were broken, as though he'd been scrabbling to pull himself up. The man took the mug, still full of tea, from Father's hands.

"Now you help Irwyn take Henry home." the man said. He led Father to the cart and placed one of his hands on a handle. Father grasped it without a word. The man turned to me. "Maybe I should come with you," he said.

I shook my head. "We'll look after him." I choked out the words as I clutched the other handle. "They need you here."

We had no lantern and clouds hid the moon but we knew the way by heart. We pushed Henry up the hills then walked in front of the cart, so it wouldn't get away from us, on the way down. I kept hearing that second cry, before everything went black in the mine. Had my hat with its burning candle made Henry fall? Surely if he'd fallen from the ladder, his body would have been a mess. Unless he'd landed in water. He should never have made me follow him into the mine. He knew I was terrified.

Father didn't say a word. When we reached our cottage, he went inside and sat in Mother's rocking chair. The cart wouldn't fit through our doorway so I followed him inside.

"We can't leave Henry out there."

Father didn't answer.

"What if the foxes find him? Or the crows?"

He didn't even look up.

"Help me, damn you. It's not my fault."

Father rocked back and forth, staring into the empty fireplace, as he had every day since that grim December day Mother died.

I wanted to punch him. Punch something. Because deep down I knew that it *was* my fault. I hadn't had the courage to admit I couldn't go down the mine and Henry had paid the price.

We were both shivering. We needed to dry off. I left the door ajar so I could keep an eye on Henry and tried not to drip tears onto the fire I was lighting. When the twigs began to crackle, I went out to the cart, unlaced Henry's boots and took them off. Then I hooked my hands through Henry's armpits, dragged him inside and lowered him onto the pallet we shared. Was that dirt or a burn mark on his sleeve? It didn't smell burned but it was soaking wet.

He was so cold. I wanted to dry him off, warm him. His sleeve clung to his arm as I tried to peel it off. I jerked harder than I needed to pull it free, willing him to sit up and pin my arms behind my back the way he had when my childish roughhousing grew annoying. But of course he couldn't. His trousers were easier. His neck was already stiffening as I stared at the bruises on his temple and chest. The arm with the broken fingernails was scraged too. I tucked him in his blanket, then hung his shirt and trousers on pegs to dry. I was so tired I could barely see straight. I stripped off my own clothes, hung them up and curled under my blanket. I should have made Father take off his wet clothes but it was too much effort to get up again.

A lifetime later there was a knock on our door. It opened and Mr. Gribble held up a candle as he leaned on his stick and looked around the room.

"Go and help Mary with breakfast," he said.

My work clothes were still wet and muddy so I pulled on my Sunday best. After Mother died, Mrs. Gribble had insisted we eat our meals with them.

"Ain't no harder to feed six than it is to feed three," she'd said.

So Father gave her part of our wages and the Gribbles' daughter, Mary, who didn't work at the mine because of a crooked leg, cooked for us all.

When I entered their cottage, Mrs. Gribble gave me the once-over and told me to fetch a bucket of water. I padded across dewy grass to the pump. My feet were wet and I saw I'd forgotten to put on my boots. Candles were lighting up the other homes as I lugged the full bucket back to the Gribbles' cottage. Mrs. Gribble warmed a bowl of water with some from her boiling kettle and gave me a piece of soap.

"Clean the mud off your face and feet. Better wash your hair too."

I did as I was told and by the time I'd towelled my hair dry, Mary had ladled generous dollops of barley gruel into bowls. Mrs. Gribble poured mugs of tea, stretched for a brandy bottle on a high shelf and poured some into the tea.

My hand shook as I reached for a spoon and I realized I hadn't eaten since breakfast the day before.

"Now drink this up," said Mrs. Gribble, sliding a mug of tea towards me. "You've had a shock and it will warm you up. I'll take these for your father."

She left carrying a mug of brandy tea and a bowl of hot gruel. She knew that Father didn't hold with liquor and never drank any, but I didn't say anything. Mugs of tea were never wasted and someone would drink it. I sipped mine and a warm glow spread through my chest.

"If the captain smells brandy on my breath, he'll fire me," I said to Mary as she stirred her gruel with her spoon. Not that this would matter anyway. I'd never be able to work underground. But I did need a job. Especially if Father's strangeness got worse and he couldn't work. In the space of a few weeks my family of almost five had shrunk to two. And not even a whole two. A blob of gruel dripped from my spoon onto the table and I stared at it.

"Father says they can't work the mine until they've pumped out all the water," Mary said. "Four of the missing men have been found alive. Seven are still unaccounted for. The rest…" She flashed a look at me. "There will be burials to arrange and…" Mary paused then reached across the table and squeezed my arm. "I'm so sorry."

She stood abruptly and swept her bowl into the washing up pail, but not before I'd seen the tears in her eyes. I swallowed hard and went to feed our pigs.

The pigs jostled and grunted around their trough. A shaft of sunlight lit up the back wall of the sty. On a ledge was a little wooden horse and cart that Father had carved for my fourth birthday. He'd been different then. Always whistling or humming. When he wasn't at the mine he kept busy carving clothes pegs or chairs or whatever else we needed. The wheels on the cart really turned and the horse had a silly grin that showed its teeth. I'd meant to give it to my baby brother. If only he hadn't got tangled up in his cord, then perhaps Mother wouldn't have burned up with fever. But Father and I had begun arguing about me not wanting to be a miner long before then.

I was wondering how pigs felt about losing a brother or sister when Charley Pascoe, my best friend, hopped over the front wall of the sty. Patches, who followed him everywhere, yipped to let us know she was stuck outside, her legs too short to jump over the wall.

"Anyone looking for me?" I asked, as Charley lifted Patches into the sty then sat beside me in the straw. Charley and Father were the only people left who knew this was my favourite place to think.

"No." Charley shook his head and handed me a pasty still warm from the oven. It didn't taste of anything but I ate it because it gave me an excuse not to talk. I usually told Charley everything, but I couldn't tell him what had happened at the mine. And Charley wasn't the kind to talk if he had nothing to say so we sat in silence for a while.

"You ever think of working somewhere else?" I asked, as Patches licked the last crumbs from my lap.

"Where?" Charley wasn't much of a dreamer.

"Anywhere. What if you could be anything you wanted?"

"What's wrong with farming?" Charley asked. "We might not have money in our pockets but we always having something to fill our bellies."

"But what if you hated it and your uncle offered you a job with people that travelled all over the country but your Father didn't want you to take it. What would you do?"

Charley shrugged. "What are *you* going to do?" he asked.

"I don't know. Why does Father get so angry when I say I want to work in my uncle's inn?"

"You could go anyway. He can't stop you."

But there was no one else to look after him now. And there was the promise I'd made Mother. Charley was lucky. He liked working in the fields with his father and brothers, and farmers didn't have to climb down into the suffocating bowels of the earth.

* * *

Two of Henry's many friends watched over him while Father and I ate supper with the Gribbles. When we returned to our cottage, Father resumed rocking in Mother's chair without saying anything. I shivered. We hadn't lit a fire because we had to keep Henry cool. The women had washed him and stitched him into a sheet ready for burial the next day. A cloth tied around his chin held his mouth shut. Pennies held his eyelids closed over eyes that would never wink at me again as we shared a joke. The pennies also paid the ferryman to take the body across the river to the world of the dead, so Henry wouldn't be left to wander, but this was something we didn't talk about when the vicar was around.

"It's hard to believe, Henry being drowned like that," said John, the more talkative friend. He straightened a sprig of rosemary placed on Henry's chest to keep away the smell of death.

"Yeah," said George, the quiet one. "He always left a piece of his lunchtime pasty for the knockers."

"But him being a blaster, I mean," said John.

"It's a dangerous job," I said.

"Even with the new safety fuses," agreed John. "But Henry was careful. He hadn't so much as an earlobe or a fingertip blown off. And then he had to go and drown. Poor blighter."

"He would've drowned quickly," said George, patting my shoulder.

I glanced towards Henry's broken fingernails, now tidied up like the rest of him.

When his friends had gone, I ruffled Henry's hair, straw-coloured like mine, around the chin cloth so it looked more like he always wore it. I left a candle burning. Father's endless rocking, which had seemed so comforting when I was a youngster curled into Mother's lap, was creepy.

Chapter 4

The ponderous knell of our church bell echoed across the fields, tolling the age of each man and boy about to be buried. Uncle Glen hadn't arrived yet but several of Henry's friends had gathered outside our cottage. They helped lift a stiff and pale Henry into the coffin that Jory, the carpenter, had delivered onto the handcart.

Father still hadn't uttered a word but he grasped one of the handles and together we wheeled Henry on his final journey to the church with the Gribbles and Henry's friends following silently behind. Sparrows still flitted through the hedgerows, the sun played in and out of the clouds, and a farmer whistled to his dog as if nothing had changed.

The cart wheels creaked as we made our way along Church Lane. Inside the gateway, we lifted Henry's coffin from the cart and rested it on the coffin stone. The vicar strode down the path to greet us. Henry's friends steadied his coffin on their shoulders. For once, I was glad I was too short to help.

"I am the resurrection and the life…" began the vicar, and we followed him into the church.

Uncle Glen, my mother's brother, wasn't there. I looked for him as more mourners arrived, the men bearing coffins, their women following behind. Then it hit me. Uncle Glen didn't know. With his strange mood upon him, Father hadn't sent a message. I should have thought of it. I closed my eyes to hide my tears.

Without the usual whispered greetings and chatter, the church was eerily quiet. Some of the men slapped Father on the shoulder as they passed. Hanna squeezed my hand. Mrs. Gribble gave me a hug followed by one of her searching looks. A loud and awkward scrimmage to make room for one more coffin distracted us and saved me from the humiliation of tears.

"This way," hissed the verger as two men helped him push Henry's coffin nearer to the one beside it. As they did so, something caught my eye. I was about to take a closer look but Mrs. Gribble grabbed my hand and led me to a space on the front pew beside Father. Images of Mother's December burial began to flash through my head. Was this really happening? Was Henry really dead or was I going crazy?

I stood and sat with the rest of the congregation. I heard them sing. I waited. When it was time to move outside, I slid out of our pew, walked over to Henry's coffin, and placed my hand over the heart-shaped knot in the wood. I looked back to the space beside Father where Henry should have been. No, I wasn't going crazy. Henry was dead. So what was going on?

Henry's friends carried him out to an open grave dug next to Mother and the baby. I didn't want to think about them being beneath the ground, unable to breathe. But that was stupid. They didn't need to breathe anymore. I'd never asked Henry if he was scared of anything. There were a lot of things I'd never be able to ask him now.

"Man that is born of woman hath but a short time to live…" intoned the vicar.

When he'd finished, Father and I each threw a handful of earth onto the coffin. Then I slipped away. The Gribbles would look after Father and I couldn't handle one more person feeling sorry for me. Not when Henry's death was all my fault.

Chapter 5

I was half way home when I heard footsteps running along behind me. There were no nearby bushes to duck behind.

"Wait for me," someone called.

It was Charley. I turned and tried to smile but it felt wrong.

"I didn't see you leave the churchyard," said Charley.

I shrugged and turned to walk on. Charley fell into step beside me and we walked in silence while I decided what to tell him.

"There was something strange about Henry's coffin," I said.

"Strange how?"

"It had a knot in the wood the same shape as the knot in Mother's coffin."

"Lots of trees have knots."

"Not heart-shaped ones."

Charley was quiet for a moment.

"It was probably made from the same tree."

"But the knot was exactly the same size and so were two small holes in the lid. If they were different planks from the same tree the knot and holes would have been bigger or smaller, so how come they're exactly the same size and in exactly the same places on the coffin?"

"I dunno," said Sam.

"It was the same coffin."

Sam whistled. "How can it be?" he asked. "It's been two months since your mother was buried."

It had been exactly ten weeks but I didn't correct him.

"It would be dirty," Charley continued, "and…

He trailed off as we turned to stare at each other.

"Maybe Jory dug it up soon after it had been buried, to use it again?" I said.

"It might not be Jory."

Jory our carpenter was a tall man capable of hefting whole tree trunks. He'd been at the service. I pictured his face again. He hadn't looked as though he'd been working nonstop for the last two nights and days to turn out enough coffins for everyone.

"But he must know," I said. "Even if it'd been cleaned up, he'd wonder about someone wanting to sell him a coffin."

Charley always bit his lip when he was thinking. "You think he comes back after the burial?" he asked.

"And digs up the coffin," I said.

"Puts the body back in the grave."

"And cleans off the coffin for next time."

"It's not right," said Charley. "You have to do something."

"Like what?"

"Tell the constable."

"You think he'll believe me?" I asked.

"I'm not sure *I* believe you," said Charley.

"Then how else can you explain the markings? It wasn't just the knots. The wood was darker and lighter in all the same places."

Charley bit his lip again. "You need proof," he said, after a few moments. "He'd have to do it at night."

I'd had more time to think about this than Charley had. "We should go and watch," I said. "Early. It would take him the whole night to dig up all those coffins."

"We?" said Charley.

"The constable's more likely to believe two of us."

"I suppose so, but I'll have to see to the animals first."

"Of course. I'll be behind the holly bushes between the cemetery hedge and Henry's grave. We should be able to see from there."

"Right," said Charley. "I'd better go then." He turned away then back again. "Oh, I almost forgot. You know the butcher's shop this side of town?"

"What about it?" I asked.

"I heard his boy left."

"Where'd he go?"

"Headed north to get a job laying railway lines."

A hawk swooped from a nearby fence post and grabbed something small in its talons.

"How much do you think the butcher's boy earned?" I asked.

"Dunno, but I have to clear stones out of a new field. I'd better get started if I'm meeting you in the churchyard later. Bye."

Charley turned and ran back the way we'd come. The mention of stones gave me an idea. I found three with distinctive markings, slipped them into my pocket, then turned my thoughts to the butcher's shop as I continued on. I was used to dealing with pigs. I'd butchered the last couple of litters all by myself. Father wouldn't be happy to hear I was leaving the mine but I'd still live at home where I could keep an eye on him. Besides, I was on borrowed time at the mine. The captain would want to fill the dead miners' shifts as soon as the mine was pumped dry and workable.

I couldn't go to see the butcher today though. I might not be back in time to hide before Jory began his sneaking night's work in the churchyard. It wasn't right, selling coffins over and over. Some families could barely scrape together the money to pay for a coffin. And there would be nothing to stop the earth from pressing against Henry's eyes and mouth and nose. I shuddered.

* * *

Mary never complained about her crooked leg but I could tell from her limp that it was aching and it took forever for her to wash up after supper. I finished my job of drying the dishes, flung the tea towel over its hook to dry and set off for the churchyard, wondering what to do if I was right about Jory.

Clouds covered the moon but the dark night didn't scare me like the suffocating blackness of the mine. I slowed down as I approached the churchyard and peered ahead. Would Jory risk using a lantern? It would be hard for him to see what he was doing without one. I stopped to listen for the sounds of a spade clanking against stony soil but the wind ruffled leaves and set tree branches swaying and creaking. If I couldn't hear him, at least he wouldn't hear me either. Avoiding the path, I scrambled over the hedge then listened again before creeping towards the bushes near Henry's grave.

Was that Charley? That dark shape? I didn't want to spook him.

"Charley?" I whispered.

He didn't answer. I crept closer and whispered again.

"Charley."

He didn't move. Hoping he wouldn't yell, I reached out and touched … stone. Things really look different at night. Obviously I was the first one there, as I'd intended, but I hoped Charley wouldn't be long. I sat on a flat stone then stood up again in case I had to move quickly. I buttoned up my jacket against the cold wind and waited.

Chapter 6

A dark shape swooped past, barely clearing my head. I ducked, my heart racing, but it was only an owl silently scouting for food. There were rustlings too. Probably the wind but I wished Charley was with me. I knelt on a clump of damp grass to rest my legs and must have dozed off because I came to with a jerk, my mouth dry. What was that? Not the wind, although it was picking up. It would be just my luck for it to rain. The noise came again. The huff of a horse. I peered through the bushes and saw draft horses harnessed to a wagon full of … what? How long had I been asleep? And where was Charley? It wasn't like him to break his word.

A soft thud sounded. I froze and listened. There, it came again … and again. I stretched towards a higher gap in the bushes. The thuds were spadefuls of earth being tossed to the ground. Someone was digging but a headstone blocked my view. Goosebumps ran down my arms. I glanced over to Henry's grave. Not his then. Not yet, anyway. I struggled to stand, my feet heavy with the cold, and lumbered towards a bigger gap in the bushes. There were two men. The tall one *was* Jory, I was sure. There weren't many men in Redruth with shoulders that wide. But who was the other? Their lantern on the ground left their faces in shadow.

The men piled earth beside the grave. I shivered and wished I was home tucked up in my blanket. It seemed ages before Jory threw down his spade, pried with a crowbar and lifted a coffin lid out onto the ground. The two men struggled to pull the corpse up, feet first. Another struggle and they had the coffin out of the hole. They began hefting lumps from the wagon that clunked together like rocks as they landed in the grave. Next they shoveled the earth back into the grave. But they'd forgotten the corpse. They stomped the earth down and shone the lantern over the gravesite. Surely they must have seen the body lying on the ground. They loaded the empty coffin onto the cart. Then, grunting with the effort, they hoisted the corpse onto the cart too.

What were they going to do with it? The wind blew a soggy leaf into my mouth. I spat it out and snapped my jaw shut. Were they stealing bodies as well as coffins?

I had to find out who the second man was. He reached for the lantern and I stepped forward to get a better look at him. I cried out as my foot plunged down a hole and I sprawled into scratchy holly branches. I froze.

"Who's there?" cried a voice I'd heard before. But whose was it?

Something growled and tugged at my boot down the hole. I grabbed a thick stem, pulled myself upright and yanked my foot out of the hole. It came with a badger clamped to the toe of my boot.

"Show yourself."

The voice was closer. My scratched hands smarted as I tried to shake off the badger. It clung on.

"What the devil?"

My mystery man held the lantern up to my face and lit up his own. Dr. Basset!

"It's the Tremayne boy," said the doctor.

The badger growled again and Dr. Basset lowered the lantern to reveal a very pissed off badger. Luckily it wasn't fully grown. Even so, it would have made a mess of my toes if my boots hadn't been too big. Jory lifted his spade and sliced it down across the badger's neck. It's jaw unclamped and it slumped to the ground. Jory threw down his spade, grabbed my arm in a grip I wasn't going to wriggle out of, and twisted my arm behind my back.

"What are you doing here?" asked the doctor. He kicked the badger but it didn't respond. He picked it up and flung it into the bushes.

"Looking for … money. It fell through a hole in my pocket. This morning."

Money? I couldn't believe I'd said that.

FRANCES HERN

"You're looking for money in the middle of the night with no lantern?" asked Dr. Basset. His voice was thick as though he had a bad cold.

"He's lying," said Jory.

As if it wasn't obvious. Why couldn't I do just one thing right? Jory yanked my arm tighter and I swallowed a yelp of pain.

"He's spying on us," said Jory.

"Why would I be spying on you?"

"None of your business," said Jory, trying to twist my arm out of its socket.

His mouth curled into a cruel smile and all the anger and frustration I'd been holding inside burst out of me along with words I couldn't control.

"It *is* my business. My brother was buried here this morning and you're not digging *him* up."

There was silence as my words hung in the air and I wished I could take them back. Jory's grin turned into a scowl

"You won't be so bold when we bury you in one of these graves," he spat out with a gust of rancid breath.

"No need to do that," said the doctor. "He won't tell anyone what he's seen."

"How do you know?"

The doctor sneezed and snorted a wad of snot to the ground before answering.

"Because, if he does, I'll have his father committed to Bodmin asylum."

Bodmin! Where inmates bit off each other's ears and fingers. Where they were strapped down for so long they lost the use of their legs. Where they were drugged to keep them quiet.

"You can't do that," I yelled. "My father's not mad."

"That's not what people are saying", the doctor said. "They say he doesn't speak anymore. Just rocks in his chair and stares into space. They say he lost his mind when your mother died."

No!

"Then what *are* we going to do with him?" asked Jory.

The clouds had begun to spit hailstones. They stung my hands and face and slid down the back of my neck. I tried not to look afraid as Dr. Basset studied my face in the lantern light.

"Let him go," said the doctor.

"Let him go?" repeated Jory, as though he couldn't believe what Dr. Basset had just said.

"I've had enough for one night." said Dr. Basset.

"But what about the other graves?" asked Jory.

"If we continue working in this weather we'll leave muddy prints and cart tracks for everyone to see. Let's take what we've got. The boy can go home."

"You sure he won't tell on us?"

"I won't let you lock Father up in the asylum," I said.

"Good," said the doctor. "That's settled then."

They took another look around the empty gravesite, threw their spades into the cart, climbed aboard, and steered the horses back to the road.

I walked over to Henry's grave, took the three stones from my pocket and squatted. Hot tears dripped from the end of my nose. Oh, Henry. Everything was going wrong. I placed one stone where his head lay, one at his feet and one over his heart, then pushed them into the wet earth so they wouldn't be easily dislodged.

As I hurried home, the hail turned into driving rain. I slipped into our cottage and quickly closed the door. Mother's rocking chair creaked behind me and my relief at being home drained away.

"Stop it, Father." I leaned against the back of the chair so it wouldn't rock. "People think you're crazy." "It helps me," he said. "Where've you been?"

Surprised to hear him speak, I blurted out "the Gribbles." I couldn't possibly have got so wet running the thirty or forty paces from the Gribbles' cottage but Father didn't look at me. If he had, perhaps I'd have told him where I'd really been. As it was, he lay down on his pallet and pulled up his blanket. At least he was going to sleep in his bed tonight. That was something.

I hung my wet clothes over Mother's washing tub and toweled myself dry. The holly scratches on my face stung but there was no blood on the towel where I dabbed at them. I lay down and rolled up in my blanket. Who would believe me if I told them what I'd seen? Doctors were educated. Respected. And how could I tell anyone anyway? I'd already killed my brother. I couldn't send Father to the lunatic asylum.

Chapter 7

I woke to find Father standing over me. To my amazement, he was washed, brushed, and wearing his coat.

"I'm off to a meeting in town," he said, as if there was nothing unusual about this. "I'll be back by supper time."

Talk about flabbergasted. He'd closed the door behind him before I could splutter "meeting? What meeting?"

I pulled on my shirt. If I ran and caught up to him, we could walk into Redruth together but I'd have to go with an empty stomach, and I couldn't face another argument about me not wanting to work down the mine. I went to see what Mary was cooking for breakfast.

* * *

The February sun broke through the clouds as I walked into Redruth. Maybe it would be safe to report Doctor Basset and Jory if Father's strange moods didn't come back.

45

The doctor couldn't lock someone up without good reason. Or could he? And what had happened to Charley last night?

As I neared the butcher's shop, I thought about what I was going to say. I tried a few words out loud.

"Good afternoon sir. I heard you were looking for an assistant."

Hmmm. Assistant sounded a bit grand for someone who'd be sweeping the floor and scrubbing blood and guts off the chopping block. But I wanted to sound confident. I needed this job.

"This is your lucky day, sir. I am your new butcher's boy."

No. That was too confident. But if I sounded desperate he might lower the wages.

"I'm looking for work, sir. I'm fourteen years old, I learn quickly and I know how to butcher pigs."

That might do. It sounded polite and businesslike. I muttered it to myself a couple more times then knocked on the shop door. When I knocked a third time, more loudly, a voice shouted, "We're closed."

I banged again. A balding man opened the door part way and waved a muscular arm.

"Clear off. I've had enough of you boys playing tricks on me when you think I'm not looking".

"But I'm here for a job."

"A job?" "Butcher's boy. I heard your boy left to work on the railway and I work at the mine but I hate it and I've butchered pigs and I don't mind the blood and guts and I'll work really hard because I don't want to go down the mine."

"Butcher's boy, eh?" He looked me up and down. "Come in."

Feeling encouraged, I followed him through the shop.

"Lift that down for me."

He nodded at a carcass hanging from the ceiling. Cows look really big close up. Much bigger than pigs. But I could do this. I reached up and tried to lift it off its hook. Nothing happened. I moved my hands so I could make more of a lifting motion but still couldn't unhook it. I hugged the carcass as though it was Charley's smashing sister, Tamsin. Then I bent my knees and jumped up. The hook came free. Yes!

As my feet touched the floor, the carcass and I began to stagger across it like dance partners with four left feet. Then my knees buckled. I threw out a hand to save us and sent a row of butcher's knives crashing to the floor. Next thing I knew, I was lying on my back amongst knives and sawdust still hugging the clammy, fleshy-smelling carcass to my chest with one arm.

The butcher grunted as he hauled the carcass off me, hung it back up, and flicked sawdust from it with a cheesecloth rag. I stood up and gathered the knives, making a show of lining them up along the counter until I had no excuse to avoid the butcher's gaze.

"Sorry," I said, expecting a right basting but the corners of his mouth twitched. Was he trying not to laugh?

"Come back when you've grown muscles," he said.

I could only nod.

"The tannery's always looking for workers" said the butcher.

I nodded again and closed the shop door behind me. I knew why the tannery was always short of workers. But I was more than half way there and I needed a job. Besides, if they were short of people, the wages might be good.

I set off past market stalls that yesterday would have been selling everything from pilchards to clothes pegs and pianos. The stalls were empty today, but a fishy smell lingered. The smell grew more putrid as I drew closer to the tannery, reminding me of a bloated dead rabbit I'd once come across in the woods. Perhaps I'd get used to it.

I opened the tannery gate. A grey-faced man with a swollen-looking body came out of one of the buildings

"What d'you want?" he called.

"I'm looking for work," I called back.

He grunted and waved me over. The stench of rotting hides grew stronger. I swallowed hard.

"How old are you?"

"Fourteen."

I tried breathing through my mouth.

"Ever worked in a tannery before?"

I shook my head. As we walked towards a shed, I kicked something. A rat. A very dead rat. Maggots plopped on my boot. My fried egg breakfast began to churn. The maggots were moist and squirmy. I slapped a hand over my mouth and ran.

I'd missed out on two jobs in one day. God forbid I should end up in the workhouse. Perhaps I *should* leave for Truro. Uncle Glen had promised me work. I could just go one morning before Father was awake. Leave him a note. It might shake him out of his moods. He'd snapped out of it this morning when he wanted to go somewhere. Without me. It wasn't a Methodist meeting or he'd have invited me along. So where on earth had he gone?

The tannery smell followed me home as I decided I *would* go. Tomorrow morning. As soon as I could get away without having to explain to Father, or the Gribbles. I should have done so weeks ago. If I had, Henry … I took a deep breath. There was no point going there. I couldn't undo Henry's death. At the pump, I washed my hands and face but the smell lingered so I ducked my head beneath it and scrubbed water through my hair. When I reached our cottage, Charley was leaning against the pigsty wall.

"Sorry about last night," he said. "I had to help with a couple of sheep that were lambing. Did you see anything?"

I shook my head unable to meet his gaze.

"Nothing at all? How long did you wait?"

"Ages."

"So we still can't explain the knots on Henry's coffin."

To change the subject I told Charley about my visit to the butcher. I tottered about hugging an imaginary beast. It felt good to laugh.

"How long before the captain sends you underground?" asked Charley, when we'd stopped laughing.

"He's lost thirty-nine men. He'll want to replace them."

"So what are you going to do?"

"Work for my Uncle Glen."

"In Truro? What about your father?"

I shrugged. When the captain found out I was too scared to go down the mine, he'd fire me. And everyone would hear. Gossip travelled faster than runaway horses. But Father would *have* to let me work elsewhere.

"I'm glad we were wrong about Jory," said Charley. "After church, the vicar's nephew helped me read an article about body snatching and it was creepy. He asked why you weren't there. Said your reading and handwriting won't improve if you don't practice."

"Body snatching?"

"Here."

Charley handed me a piece of torn newspaper. I stared at the headline trying to make out the words: *med i cal stu dents buy bo dies.*

Chapter 8

"What's that funny smell?" asked Mrs. Gribble, when I went in for supper.

I quickly slid along the bench to the far end of the table. Mr. Gribble picked up my boots I'd left by the door and sniffed at them. I half expected him to ask about the badger punctures but before he could speak, Father burst in.

"Hope I haven't kept you waiting," he said. He didn't mention where he'd been until we'd eaten and Mary began to gather our supper dishes.

"Leave them a minute, Mary. I've something to say," he said. "Irwyn and I are leaving."

A knife slid from Mary's pile and clanged to the floor.

"Leaving?" Mrs. Gribble looked as shocked as I felt.

"We're going to the Virgin Islands."

Where?

"We'll work our month's notice at the mine and leave the first of April."

Yes! Dr. Basset wouldn't be able to send Father to the lunatic asylum.

"I'll be sorry to leave you behind, Jago. You've been the best partner a man could want, especially over recent weeks, but I think it's best."

I wouldn't have to find another job. And no one would know what a coward I was.

"I've never heard of no Virgin Islands," said Mrs. Gribble.

"They're across the sea," said Father. "We'll travel by ship."

Sail. Me. Across the sea. I'd never left Cornwall, let alone England.

"What will you do there?" asked Mr. Gribble.

"Work the copper mine on one of the islands."

"No." It came out loudly and everyone stared at me. "I can't work underground."

"It won't be like working here," said Father. "There won't be mud and flash floods and horrible memories. We'll leave them behind and start afresh."

"It's not memories I'm afraid of. It's not being able to see or breathe. Not knowing where I am."

"You'll soon learn your way around. Everything will be fine, you'll see. Besides, it's all arranged. I've signed the contract."

"If Irwyn don't want to go, he can stay with us," said Mrs. Gribble.

"But the captain will move him underground," said Father.

"No. I'll go and work for Uncle Glen," I said.

Father looked at me long and hard then strode out of the cottage. I grabbed my boots, rushed outside, thrust my feet into them, and yanked the laces tight. I looked up in time to see the door to our cottage close. I ran, concentrating on foxholes and tree roots that might trip me. I ran until my breath came in ragged gasps then sank onto a granite boulder. Why hadn't Father told me about this before? Had he even considered I might not want to go? And what if I didn't, would it make trouble for him? If it did, it was his fault. He should have told me what he was going to do and not just announced it in front of everyone.

A breeze dried my sweat as my breathing slowed. The full moon shone on the old castle at Carn Brea and the new granite monument. They rose on the hilltop ahead like guards on the lookout. Something was clanging away at the back of my mind like the funeral bell. As I sat there, snippets from conversations with Father branded themselves on my brain.

"Wyn! Stop dreaming and pay attention," he'd say. And "be careful what you wish for Wyn, it might come true."

And had I listened? No. I'd wished Henry didn't have to work the most dangerous job in the mine. I'd wished I didn't have to work at the mine at all. And now we didn't, but at what cost!

There were rustlings in the long grass and something screeched off in the distance. Cold from the granite boulder seeped through my thinning trousers. A shiver ran through me. I stood and turned towards home. But how much longer would it be my home? Father was leaving the country and I was going to Truro. Father couldn't stop me if he wasn't here. But I'd be leaving him to sail to the ends of the earth on his own. If his strangeness returned he wouldn't be able to look after himself. I might never see him again.

Our row of whitewashed cottages shone in the moonlight. I stopped at the pump and took a long drink. Inside, Father was sitting in Mother's chair but he'd lit a candle and he wasn't rocking.

"I thought you'd be pleased," he began, when I'd closed the front door. "You've said you didn't want to work here, wanted to see other places."

He knew what I wanted. We'd argued over it often enough.

"Look, I know I haven't been much help to you lately. I promise things will get better but I can't stay here. Everywhere I look, everything I touch reminds me …" he stopped and swallowed. "At least we still have each other. Come with me, Wyn."

There were dark smudges beneath his eyes and I noticed, as if it had only just happened, that his hair was thinning to a bald patch. I wanted to say yes, I would go with him. But I couldn't work in a mine and if I told him how I was so certain, he'd know it was my fault Henry was dead. He'd hate me.

"I need to think about it," I said.

I was lying in bed with my blanket tucked under my chin when it occurred to me that Jory and Dr. Basset might return to the churchyard that night for the rest of the bodies. I should go and stop them from digging up Henry. But how? There was Dr. Basset's threat and Father wouldn't be leaving for another month. I was so tired I didn't want to get out of bed ever again. Besides, the wind was blowing up as though it was going to rain again. Perhaps bad weather would keep them away.

Father began to snore but I couldn't sleep. Perhaps I could bargain with Dr. Basset. I could promise to keep quiet if they left Henry alone. I crept out of bed and dressed as quietly as I could, so as not to wake Father.

* * *

As I approached Henry's grave something scrunched and I froze. Someone had stepped on gravel and it wasn't me. At first glance, everything looked as it had when I'd left the night before. Then a dark shape slipped behind that rock I'd thought was Charley. The shape wasn't bulky enough to be Jory. Was it Dr. Basset? But what was he doing? He had his back to me so I crept closer to the bushes I'd hidden behind yesterday and waited. He was waiting too, but for what? I was just thinking the shape looked small even for Dr. Basset when he stepped away from the rock and looked around. The moonlight shone on his face. Charley's face!

I relaxed my hunched shoulders and stepped out from the shelter of the bushes.

"Hey, Charley," I whispered. Charley turned and saw me as I snuck up beside him.

"Seen anything?"

"No," Charley whispered.

We waited in silence.

Things might have gone differently if Charley had been with me yesterday. I wished I dared tell him what happened. He could help me figure out what to do.

At one point we both heard something but it was only a fox trotting by. A long time later, we watched a hedgehog hunting for slugs and beetles.

"I don't think Jory's coming," said Charley, after yawning for the umpteenth time.

"Maybe it's too muddy," I said. "Let's call it a night."

"See you," said Charley, and he headed off towards his farm.

I knew I wouldn't sleep with my thoughts running in circles. I sat on a stone next to Henry's grave with my back to the wind.

"You shouldn't have made me go down the mine" I said to Henry. "You knew I was scared. And now you can't help me."

I hadn't gone with Uncle Glen after Mother's funeral because Father was upset and I didn't want to make him worse but if I had gone then Henry would still be alive. If only Mother hadn't died. I recalled her words to me just before the childbed fever stole her mind.

"Your father will take this very hard," she'd said," but he loves you dearly. Promise me you'll look after him."

Then I knew I didn't really have any choice, because I *had* promised. I couldn't let them lock Father up in the asylum and I couldn't leave him to sail across the world on his own.

Chapter 9

I placed a row of pebbles along the pigsty wall, one for each day until the end of March. Each morning, before breakfast, I threw one away. The mine captain said there was little point my learning a new job so I stayed in the jigging shed. Sometimes I found myself whistling, the way I used to before Mother died. At other times I wondered how I could leave the only home I'd ever known. I felt as though I was on a seesaw, trying not to bang my backside on the ground.

I butchered one of our pigs for the Gribbles and sold the rest. The empty pigsty felt cold and lonely. I tried not to worry about where I'd work when we reached the Virgin Islands. That was months away and half-way around the world. But I'd promised myself I'd do something to stop Jory and Dr. Basset.

Charley'd told me Dr. Basset had moved away but he could still be robbing graves wherever he was. Some nights I dreamt that a wagon full of mad people came to take Father to the asylum. When I tried to tell them it was a mistake, that there was nothing wrong with him, I couldn't speak. The mad people tried to pull Father away from me. They pulled off his arms and legs and threw them into the wagon so I was left holding his body and screaming head. I'd wake up to find it was me screaming and when Father asked what was wrong I couldn't tell him because I didn't want his strange moods to return.

I was sitting beside Henry's grave one evening, asking him what I should do, when an idea came to me. I turned it over in my mind for several days and the more I thought about it, the more it felt right.

The last day of March was also my last day at the mine. After supper I went over to Charley's to say goodbye. Luckily for me he was spreading fresh hay in the sheep barn by himself. I stood in the doorway, trying to decide how to tell him I hadn't been honest with him. He looked up and saw me.

"I need your help," I said.

"Yep," said Charley, even though he had no idea what kind of help.

"You know the day we buried Henry, well … Jory did come to the churchyard that night. He came with Dr. Basset and I'm sorry I couldn't tell you."

Charley's eyes opened wider but he didn't say anything, just leaned his hay fork against a post and looked at me. I told him what had happened. When I finished, Charley whistled.

"So you were right after all," he said.

"The three stones I left on Henry's grave are still there so I don't think they came back."

"It rained a lot that week," said Charley. "It was muddy."

"Just because Dr. Basset's left Redruth doesn't mean he isn't still snatching bodies though."

"Or Jory could carry on without him," added Charley. "What do you want help with?"

That was typical of Charley. I don't know why I'd thought he might get upset and refuse. I unwrapped the pen, ink and paper I'd begged from our writing session after last Sunday's church service.

"I want you to write a letter for me."

Charley didn't have to ask why. His writing was readable. Mine looked as though a drunken spider had crawled through an ink puddle. Charley wrote down what had gone on between Jory, Dr. Basset and me that night in the churchyard and then I signed the account as neatly as I could.

"Don't take it to the police until after Father and I leave tomorrow," I said.

"Don't worry. I'll keep it safe for a couple of days."

I could have hugged him but slapped his shoulder instead.

"Thanks Charley. I'll miss you."

"Not for long," said Charley. "You'll be off seeing the world."

On my way home I stopped in the churchyard to make my peace with Henry. There was no point being angry with him. He'd only been trying to help me. I said goodbye to Mother, too, although I was almost certainly talking to an empty grave.

Back in our musty-smelling pigsty, I pulled a loose stone from the corner and lifted out the wooden treasure box Father made me for my sixth birthday. While I had given most of my wages to Mother and then Mrs. Gribble, Father allowed me to keep a penny or two and these I'd hoarded. I stowed the coins in my jacket pocket. Also in the box, wrapped in a strip of cloth, was Mother's gold locket. Tiny green stones set in the front spelled out her initials and inside were locks of hair from her mother, grandmother and great-grandmother. She'd given it to me before she died. Said she wanted me to have it because we shared the same initials and the wearer was always lucky in love. I'd snipped one of her curls and added it to the others inside. I hung it around my neck and tucked it beneath my shirt. I took a last look around the pigsty then went inside to spend one final night in our cottage. It took me ages to fall asleep.

Chapter 10

"Wyn." Father was shaking me awake. "Here." He handed me a purse half-full of coins. "In case we get separated," he said. "Tie it beneath your shirt so no one knows it's there."

I added my own coins to the purse and bundled up my spare shirt and trousers, a jersey Mother had knitted, my comb, towel and a piece of soap. It was Sunday and we trod softly down to the Gribbles' so we wouldn't wake our other neighbours. Mary was cooking up a farewell feast and no one said much until we had mopped up the last puddle of egg yolk with a final mouthful of bread fried crispy in sizzling bacon fat.

"Thank you Mary," said Father, as Mrs. Gribble refilled our tea mugs. "You've done us proud. We shall miss your hearty meals."

Mary blushed with pleasure.

"It isn't too late to change your minds and stay here with us," said Mrs. Gribble looking at me, as if she knew I'd changed my mind many times over the past month.

"We've made our decision," said Father, also looking at me. "You know our reasons for leaving."

"Yes, but you don't have to go to the ends of the earth where there are cutthroats and pirates and we'll never hear from you again. You could find work in Redruth or Truro or …"

"Now then." Mr. Gribble put an arm around his wife's shoulders. "They've got good jobs waiting and the men who hired them aren't going to ship them out there only to have them murdered before they can do any work. Besides, who knows what changes we're going to see here, what with mines closing down and eighteen-year-old Victoria about to be crowned queen. What does a strip of a girl know about running a nation?"

"And speaking of going," said Father, standing up, "we'd best say goodbye."

First though we had to open up our bundles to add pasties that Mary had made for us. Then, still blushing, she gave me a quick hug. Mrs. Gribble's hug lasted longer while the men thumped each other on the back. We picked up our bundles and left to cries of "God keep you" and "safe travels" that likely woke any neighbours still asleep.

We strode into Redruth with dawn breaking around us. It was April Fool's Day and I hoped this wasn't a bad omen. If only Father hadn't signed me up to work in the Virgin

Gorda mine, I would have been excited. Father's clothes hung loosely on his gaunt frame. Three months at sea might give him time to regain the weight he'd lost since Mother died and put some colour in his white face.

The sour smell of hops from the brewery reached us as we walked beside the rusty-coloured brook that gave Redruth its name. A few people were up early dressed in their Sunday best, the women's bonnets shading their faces from the sun. We walked past rows of two-storey granite houses set back behind gardens, and on the far side of town met up with our vicar's brother and his wife who were going to visit their married daughter. They gave us a ride to Truro in their horse-drawn wagon.

"We should call in and tell Uncle Glen where we're going," I said, after they'd dropped us off.

Father's face showed his disapproval of my fun-loving uncle.

"We've a long enough journey as it is," he said. "We'd best make the most of the daylight."

Maybe he was right. If we stopped at Uncle's Inn, I might not want to leave. But would I ever see him again?

We walked on towards St. Austell. As the daylight faded, it began to rain and by the time we arrived, I was wet, tired, and hungry. We passed an inn and two men came out wafting smells of cooking meat and wood smoke.

"Let's stay here tonight," I said. It had been hours since we'd eaten our pasties.

"It's only a couple more miles to Charlestown," said Father.

"But we're not due to join our ship until tomorrow. What have you got against inns?"

"Nothing when they provide safe lodgings. It's the serving of liquor I don't agree with."

My steps slowed with my reluctance to leave the promise of a hot meal behind.

"What harm is there in drinking a little ale or gin or brandy?"

"The harm is that they take away a man's resolve. He grows so befuddled he spends all his hard-earned wages."

"Only if the man allows it. You might as well blame a good cook for making a fat man eat too much."

"Food does not addle the brain the way liquor does. My father…"

As we passed a dark passageway three figures darted out. One of them bumped into me. Reminded of Mrs. Gribble's misgivings, I expected to feel a cold blade pressed against my throat. Instead, as I stumbled, hands snaked into my pockets.

"Leave us be!" Father shouted.

He knocked one of the boys to the ground and there was a glint of metal. Fearing for my father's life, I uttered a cry and lunged towards him. But he was the one with the knife. He sliced it through the air and our second assailant ran off. The third was still clinging to me like a limpet as he tried to find something to steal. Holding onto Mother's locket around my neck, I kicked him in the shins. He grunted, let go of me, looked at Father brandishing his knife, and melted into the shadows. The boy on the ground staggered to his feet and took off after his friends. Father grabbed my arm and we ran back to the inn and burst through the doorway.

It was busy inside and no one paid attention to us as we looked around, breathing hard. I ran a shaking hand down my middle and was relieved to feel the bump of my purse still in place.

"You win," Father said into my ear, so I would hear him over the din and clatter. "We'll stay here tonight."

"We're almost full," the innkeeper said, "but there's a small room under the stairs with one bed, if you don't mind sharing."

We didn't. We wolfed down platters of savoury stew in a dining room too noisy for conversation then lay beneath a couple of old but clean blankets on a lumpy bed. The sight of my gentle and law-abiding father wielding a knife had surprised me. What else didn't I know about him?

"It's a good job you had that knife," I said, finally able to hold a private conversation.

"We were lucky. They were young ruffians looking to steal the price of a meal." He was quiet for a moment. "I thought about buying you a knife," he said. "But until you've filled out a bit, it might be more of a red flag to a bull than protection."

"I'd rather have a chance to defend myself than be speared like a helpless fish."

"Well, you may not have size on your side," said Father, as he patted my shoulder, "but you do have spirit and that is half the battle won."

"What were you going to tell me about Grandfather?"

"What?"

"Before we were attacked. We were talking about inns serving liquor."

"Nothing. Go to sleep."

"But I want to know."

There was a pause then a gentle snore but I'm sure he was only pretending to be asleep. He never talked about his parents even though I'd asked him many times.

The events of the evening brought sword-waving giants to my dreams. I tried to run from their lethal curved blades but gluey mud sucked at my boots and dragged me down. My mouth filled with earth and I couldn't breathe. I woke in a cold sweat gasping for air. Mrs. Gribble's concerns about cutthroats and pirates might not have been foolish after all.

Chapter 11

Father rose early next morning and wouldn't stop for breakfast. We walked past shop windows full of china and porcelain as the salty tang of the sea grew stronger. Close up, the ocean was alive with swells and spray and waves that sucked in and out along the shore. The thought that we would sail on it for three months before we reached the Virgin Islands made my head spin. I leaned into the wind and watched squawking gulls dip and circle as we made our way to the shipping office in Charlestown harbour to ask about the Fortuna.

"She's anchored out there," said a clerk, waving a hand in the direction of the harbour. "Sails on the evening tide. Be aboard by five bells."

Father and I exchanged glances.

"How do we get aboard?" I asked.

The clerk sighed, making it clear we were interrupting his work.

"Wait for one of her boats to pull up to the quay and tell the men you're passengers."

"Let's eat breakfast while we wait," I said, my stomach rumbling.

We sat on stools at a stall and chewed on boiled whelks sprinkled with salt and vinegar. Nearby a woman selling crabs haggled with customers, shouting over the clanging and banging from the ship-building yards. Fishermen were cleaning and mending nets. Men scurried between warehouses and the quayside, some wheeling handcarts loaded with barrels and crates. Small boats ferried between anchored sailing ships and the shore. I squinted into the rising sun but couldn't make out names on the ships.

When we'd eaten, Father bought a loaf and wedge of cheese for later then led me into a chandlery.

"You sell daggers?" he asked the man behind the counter.

The man rummaged in a cabinet full of telescopes and instruments I wasn't familiar with.

He laid three knives on the counter.

"Well?" said Father, looking at me.

So it *was* for me. I picked one up. Its bone handle curved into my palm as though it belonged there. The blade looked wickedly sharp.

"This one," I said.

"How much," asked Father, then sucked in his breath when the man told him.

"That includes the leather sheath and belt," said the man, producing these items from beneath the counter.

I slipped the dagger into its sheath, fastened the belt around my waist, and held it to stop it from sliding over my hips.

"I can punch extra holes," said the man. "There'll be lots of growing room."

Father looked at me and I gave him an enthusiastic nod.

"Very well," he said.

The man used a piece of chalk to mark where to make new holes and disappeared into a back room.

"Thank you," I said.

"Just you be careful with it."

We looked around the shop while we waited. Father picked up a metal jug.

"We might need something to hold water on board," he said.

He found a tin mug too. A couple of slates caught my eye. I would have nothing to do for the next three months. If my writing were neater, and I could read a little faster, and add and subtract numbers, then perhaps I could work in the Virgin Gorda mine's office.

"If I had a slate," I said, "I could work on my handwriting."

Father could barely sign his own name but he believed in people improving themselves.

"It can't do any harm," he said.

The chandler reappeared. I fastened my belt into one of the new holes while he found some chalk to go with our slate and Father paid him. As we sauntered back towards the sea, two men pulled their boat alongside the quay and tossed a rope loop over one of numerous wooden posts.

"Are you from the Fortuna?" Father asked.

"Nope," said one of the men, as he hopped ashore. He pointed to another boat being rowed in. "They are."

The men in this second boat gave a final heave on their oars, folded them into the boat and swung neatly alongside the quay.

"We need a ride out to the Fortuna," said Father, as the men stepped ashore.

"We're busy loading cargo and provisions," said one of them. "We'll take passengers at three o'clock."

"Please sir, which ship is the Fortuna?" I asked, before he could walk away.

He pointed. "Dark green packet, third from the right." He turned and strode to catch up with the others. The Fortuna didn't have an ornately carved figure on the front like some of the other ships but she looked solidly built and had three tall masts with furled sails.

"I wonder what her cargo is?" I said to Father. "She doesn't look very big for forty miners and crew."

"I don't suppose there'll be a lot of room," said Father, "but we'll manage. Other people do."

I'd been so focussed on leaving the mine, and wondering where Dr. Basset had gone and why, that only now did it occur to me I might never set foot on Cornish soil again.

"Do you think we'll ever come back?" I asked.

Father shrugged. "Let's find somewhere to sit and wait," he said.

"We could go for a walk along the beach."

Father stared into the distance for a few moments then said, "You go. I don't much feel like it."

I turned away but perhaps he sensed my disappointment.

"I'm sorry Wyn. It's just that the last time I walked along a beach was with your mother and ..." He trailed off, then cleared his throat. "I'll sit here with our packs. Make sure you're back in time."

"Don't worry."

I wandered along the pebbly beach poking into tide pools to send crabs scurrying and watch white and pink creatures wave tentacles back and forth. It was a lovely spring day. I reached some boulders and sat down, remembering the Sunday afternoon walks the four of us used to take. Mother would pack a food basket and we'd pretend we were pirates and hunt for birds' nests and other treasure. How I'd loved those afternoons. And now I was about to sail to the Virgin Islands on a real adventure. If only Mother and Henry were coming too.

Waves fizzed and foamed over the stones, then drained out only to wash back in again with a rhythmic swoosh, in and out, in and out, in and …

Something tickled my hand. Water! Where was I? I opened my eyes. Oh yes, the beach. Waiting for our ship to sail. Our ship! The thought of the Fortuna jolted me fully awake. How long had I been asleep? What time was it?

I scrambled to my feet and looked out to where the Fortuna was anchored. Sails billowed low on two masts. Was she swinging on her anchor or leaving? I couldn't tell.

Part Two
The Fortuna

Chapter 12

The tide was in and the boulder I had fallen asleep on was half submerged. My heart thumped as I yanked off my boots and stepped into swirling water. Sharp shells sliced my feet as I sloshed through the waves. I slipped on slimy seaweed and slammed my shins into a submerged rock. Soaked from my armpits down, I set off again.

What if I didn't reach the Fortuna in time? Stupid. Stupid. Stupid. The word pounded through my brain as I staggered along, desperately wanting to be on that ship.

I slipped again and dropped my boots into the surf as I banged the same bruised line across my shins on another rock. I wiped away tears and grabbed a boot as the other was sucked out of reach. I lunged after it. A new wave broke and my boot disappeared from sight. I felt along the bottom. Couldn't see through the murky water, the waving weed. Couldn't find it. Couldn't let the ship sail without me. I had to get back to the quay. I rammed my foot into the boot I held, yanked the lace tight then tried to run, my boot filling with water as I stubbed bare toes. I stumbled towards shore.

A ship's boat with a couple of wooden crates and one man inside was alongside the quay, its line looped over a low post. Another man - Father - was seated on the post. A third man was struggling to haul him off and free the line. I was out of the sea now, running across shingle that caved in with each step, my thighs burning, the three men shouting.

"Father!" I gasped, as I squelched my way to the boat. He stood up, grabbed me by the neck of my jacket and pushed me into the boat, almost falling on top of me. The boat rocked so violently it would have turned right over if the sailor inside hadn't grabbed hold of the dock. The other sailor let fly the most amazing string of curses I'd ever heard as he flipped the rope free then stepped nimbly into the boat. The sailors rowed as fast as they could towards the Fortuna.

"They were going to leave without you," Father spat out as I tried to catch my breath

"I didn't … hear … the church bell."

As if on cue, it began to chime.

"No, you were daydreaming as usual. What was I supposed to do? If I'd gone to find you they'd have left both of us behind."

The fifth and final chime died away.

Father was still ranting as we were winched aboard, along with the crates, then the boat. When Father's strange moods were upon him, I'd have given anything to hear him speak to me. Now I was grateful for a cry of "raise the anchor." A great clanking prevented the passengers gathered along the rail from hearing more. With nowhere to go, I stood with one boot on, my bare foot scraped and bleeding. Red rivulets ran from my trouser legs across the ship's deck. It's a wonder I didn't bleed to death while Father, oblivious of my injuries, railed up one side of me and down the other. When the clanking stopped, the sailor who'd been struggling with Father on the dock bellowed for quiet and glared at us.

"I'm Mr. Reddiman, first mate, and I'm responsible for the smooth running of this ship."

Just my luck.

"As Mr. Turner calls your name, you will line up here and wait for the ship's doctor to examine you."

Examine was an exaggeration although the doctor did ask people to open their mouths and say "ahh." When he reached me, he stopped.

"Where's all this blood coming from?" he asked, peering at the deck.

"I scraped my feet on the rocks, sir."

He lifted my sodden trouser legs, holding them between thumb and forefinger as though afraid he would catch some deadly disease.

"Wait here," he said, pointing to a place beside him along the rail.

Mr. Reddiman was deep in conversation with an older man and the other sailor who'd rowed us to the Fortuna. I couldn't hear what they were saying but the sailor pointed at Father and me. I hoped there wasn't going to be trouble. The breeze picked up as we steered away from shore. Still drenched, I began to shiver.

Sailors were busy raising more sails and poking long wooden poles into every locker and space on deck. I caught a man about Henry's age looking at me. He was too well dressed to be one of the miners.

"What are they're doing, sir?" I asked, nodding towards the sailors with the poles.

"Searching for stowaways," he said.

Father was standing at the rail, staring at the rapidly shrinking Cornish coastline, his lips compressed into a tight line. I looked away again, not wanting to catch his eye. Then the doctor, carrying a bucket of water, tapped my elbow and gestured for me to follow him.

The ship was surprisingly spacious below deck. The doctor's cabin was small but cosy with a bunk, desk and cupboard all built in place. The only moveable items were a chair and two wooden chests pushed together to double as a table. Would Father and I have a cabin like this?

"Sit." The doctor pointed at one of the chests. "Wash your feet."

He placed the bucket of water in front of me as I unlaced my boot. The saltwater stung my raw, scraped feet.

"What happened to your other boot?" he asked.

"It washed away in the surf, sir."

A hint of a smile hovered around his lips.

"You're probably better off with bare feet on board ship anyway. Now let's have a look at them."

I lifted my tingling feet out of the bucket. The doctor patted them dry with a cloth and examined them. The right one wasn't bad. The left one was a mess. The doctor snipped off ragged flaps of skin, sorted some salve from amongst an array of bottles and packets in the chest I wasn't sitting on, and dabbed some onto my raw skin.

"There's no point bandaging them, the bandages will only soak up sea water but keep them clean and as dry as you can. Come back and see me if they turn red and puffy or begin to weep. Now, if you want to eat you'd better go to the dining room."

"Yes sir. Thank you."

I would have liked to change into dry clothes but didn't want to see Father until he'd calmed down. Instead, I followed my nose to a room with long tables bolted to the floor where a sailor was ladling stew into bowls. Another was handing out mugs of water. Relieved to see Father wasn't there, I sat at an empty table and ate quickly. A couple of times I looked up to see people pointing at me. I slipped out as soon as I'd eaten. Hopefully by morning they'd have something else to talk about.

Outside the dining room, I hesitated and yawned. Where could I curl up and sleep? I made my way back onto deck. The cold wind blew steadily now and there was no sign of other passengers. One of the ship's boats was stowed upside down in a cradle along the side of the deck. I wriggled underneath, where no one would see me, and wished I could talk to Charley. Was he missing me? Had he given my letter to the police yet? Perhaps the Fortuna's almost sailing without me was a sign that I shouldn't have left Cornwall after all.

I shuffled around trying to move my shoulders out of a cold draft. A dark hand shot under the side of the boat and grabbed my raw ankle. Someone began to shout.

"Lévé, lévé."

I couldn't make any sense of it and kicked hard to free my foot but another hand of a different hue grabbed my other ankle. The hands dragged me out from under the boat and someone called "fetch the captain."

A slender sailor with a strong grip hauled me to my feet. A heavier-built man grabbed my arms and held them behind my back.

"Let me go," I yelled, trying to twist free.

"You goin' over the side, boy," said the slender one. He wore a length of faded cloth wound around black chin-length hair.

"Why?" I shouted. "I haven't done anything wrong."

"What's going on?" a new voice asked.

"Stowaway, Captain." The slender sailor stood aside. The other kept my hands behind my back.

"I'm not a stowaway. You can't throw me overboard." I prayed this was true.

"Which is a great pity," said the captain, "because it would give me immense pleasure after the trouble you've caused. This … boy," he turned to the slender, dark-skinned sailor, "delayed our departure."

At his words, my hands were released and my two captors melted away. The captain's right foot, encased in a creased leather boot that reached almost to his knee, slowly tapped the rhythm of some private tune as he looked me up and down, his brow creased in displeasure.

"What's your name?"

"Irwyn Tremayne, sir."

"I hope that you are not going to cause any more trouble aboard my ship, Mr. Tremayne. I don't like trouble and I have unpleasant ways of dealing with it."

"Yes. I mean no, sir."

"Good. I shall be watching you."

"Yes sir."

With that, the captain left and I stood wondering what to do. The few sailors left on deck were busy adjusting the sails. I caught sight of a wooden locker built into the deck. It was half full of canvas bags but there was room to lie inside. I climbed in, pulled a lumpy bag out from beneath my back, placed it under my head for a pillow and lowered the lid. Although there were holes around the bottom of the locker, presumably to allow water to drain out, it cut out the wind. I pulled the canvas bags around me and feeling crept back into my toes as the rise and fall of the Fortuna's deck rocked me to sleep. Pigs grunted through my dreams.

Chapter 13

I woke, dragged from sleep by a desperate need to pee. I couldn't see a thing. Where was I? The floor beneath me plunged with a creaking of timbers and I remembered. I stretched my arms up and cracked open the lid of the locker. There was just enough light to see and I quickly untangled myself from my makeshift bed. But where could I go?

I stumbled along the deck, steadying myself as the ship rolled down the backs of waves that had grown overnight. Standing upright, I felt my bladder threaten to give way. A glance around showed only two sailors both busy with ropes. I climbed a short ladder to a low-walled deck at the front of the ship, braced myself, unbuttoned my trousers and sighed with relief as a steaming fountain arced over the side to the waves below. My sigh turned to a cry of dismay as a wind gust blew some of it back down the front of my trousers. I turned away, splashing the deck and my bare feet. Someone gasped. My head jerked up. The person — a girl? — was trotting back to the ladder.

She disappeared from view but when I climbed down the ladder a couple of minutes later, she was waiting for me.

"Never pee, spit or vomit into the wind," she said, eyeing the wet patches down my trousers.

Heat warmed my neck like a rising tide as I tried to think of something to say.

"Don't you know it's rude not to speak when you're spoken to?" she asked.

It was on the tip of my tongue to reply that I wasn't the only person being rude but she looked about my age and I was currently short of friends.

"Irwyn Tremayne," I said. "Pleased to make your acquaintance."

"Hanna Spargo."

"Are you with the miners?" I asked, wondering why I hadn't noticed her during roll call.

"No. I'm the captain's daughter."

"So he's … Captain Spargo?"

"Fathers do usually have the same name as their daughters." She paused. "I was hoping we might be friends, but you don't seem very intelligent."

"Well …" I spluttered. "You don't seem to be very polite."

To my surprise, Hanna giggled.

"That's what my aunt tells me."

"Is she on board too?"

"No, thank goodness." She tucked a stray strand of glossy, dark brown hair behind one ear. "You've never been on a ship before, have you?"

She didn't have to be highly intelligent to work that out.

"That's why I don't know where ... well ... anything is."

"The head is over there."

She pointed to a closed door.

"The head of what?" I asked.

Hanna's eyes widened. "The water closet for passengers," she said.

"And where did my father sleep last night?" I asked, to quickly change the conversation.

Hanna looked puzzled.

"Down there," she pointed again. "In steerage, but ..."

Guessing what she was going to ask, a familiar grunting noise gave me the excuse I needed to cut her off.

"Are there pigs on board?"

"In the animal pens."

So I wasn't dreaming last night.

I followed Hanna along the deck. The wind caught her skirt and I was surprised to see it was actually baggy trousers tied with a wide sash at the waist. Above the trousers she wore a loose shirt. She was a good head taller than me and her hair was pulled into a single thick plait that hung almost to her waist. We passed a coop of hens and stopped in front of narrow wooden pens with waist-high gates. Two held sows with piglets. A third held more sows. A fourth housed one of the largest boars I'd ever seen with a leather collar around his neck.

"I kept pigs back home," I said. "I always felt a bit sorry when it was time to slaughter them but Father showed me how to do it quickly, so they didn't have time to sense something bad was going to happen."

"The boar and sows with piglets belong to one of the passengers," said Hanna. "The others are ours."

"To eat?"

"And because the sailors like having them on board."

"For pets?"

Hanna laughed. Her mouth was too large for the rest of her face and showed lots of white teeth.

"No," she said, her eyes twinkling. "In case we're shipwrecked."

"So the sailors won't starve on some desert island?"

"So the sailors won't drown. They swear that pigs always swim towards the nearest shore. So if the ship sinks, the pigs will lead the sailors to land."

Could pigs smell out land? They were certainly good at sniffing out anything edible.

"Do you believe that?" asked Hanna. She still had that twinkle in her eye so I didn't know if she was teasing me.

"I don't know," I said. "I've never seen a pig swim."

"Neither have I," said Hanna. "But the captain likes to keep his crew happy. He says a happy ship is a productive ship.

We leaned our elbows on one of the half doors and watched the pigs.

"I can't swim," I said. Neither could Henry.

"Then I shall teach you."

"Where?" The grey sea churned uninvitingly.

"Closer to the islands, where it's warmer."

"Will we be able to keep up with the ship?"

"Of course not. But we're bound to stop for repairs or lose the wind for a few hours."

Perhaps Henry'd still be alive if he'd known how to swim.

My stomach gurgled. Hanna must have heard it.

"You'd best go and eat breakfast while it's hot," she said. "You're lucky. Mac's a good cook."

Before I could ask where I might find her later, she'd gone.

I made my way back to the dining room where a sailor ladled out a bowl of porridge and poured treacle on top. I sat apart from the handful of miners deep in conversation who were already eating. Father wasn't there. The porridge was satisfyingly thick and after two mouthfuls my stomach stopped rumbling. When I'd finished, I debated whether to go and tell Father breakfast was being served. I couldn't avoid him forever and now that we were on our way to Virgin Gorda, surely his temper would have improved.

Chapter 14

The sour smell of vomit hung in the air as I approached a row of bunks in a large, open area. So much for thinking we'd be in a cabin like the doctor's. There were no windows. A lantern or two cast a gloomy light and shadows that shifted as the Fortuna rode the waves. Someone groaned.

"Father?"

"Wyn. Over here."

I followed his voice to a hunched shape on one of the bunks. Our bundles of spare clothes lay on the bunk next to it.

"Where've you been?"

"I've just had breakfast. Would you like some?"

He groaned again. There was a splattering noise as someone nearby retched.

"Empty this," he said, holding out our water jug.

I caught a whiff of vomit and stale pee. My porridge churned in my stomach. I swallowed a couple of times and held the jug at arm's length.

"Do you want some water?" I asked.

"No. I want everything to stop rolling and pitching."

"Like that's going to happen," I muttered, and walked away. I turned to hear what Father called after me and skidded through a chunky puddle. My right hand shot out but found nothing to grab hold of. I went down clutching the jug as though it contained a deadly poison that would kill me instantly if so much as one drop touched my body. My tailbone smashed against the floor.

"Damn it!" I was past caring who heard me. I slid around in vomit as the Fortuna pitched up and down, and muttered every bad word I knew. When I ran out of words, I realized no one was coming to help me up. Getting up without putting my hands on the gross floor, or spilling the jug's contents, was a challenge but I managed it. So much for keeping my scraped feet clean and dry. Sour smelling chunks of half-digested food dripped down my legs as I limped to the ship's side. Relieved to be out in the bracingly fresh air, I turned my back to the wind and emptied the jug. I found a bucket with a long rope attached hanging outside the pig pens and was about to dip it into the water barrel in the dining room when a hand grasped my shoulder.

"What are you doing?"

I spun around to face a wiry man. Reddish hair streaked with grey stuck out from beneath the tartan cloth tied around his head. His left arm ended at the wrist.

"I need to wash my clothes, sir," I said.

"Aye." He wrinkled his nose. "But you'll not be wasting precious drinking water." He rolled out his r's in a strange kind of accent.

"Then how can I wash them?"

He looked at me, one eyebrow raised.

"We're surrounded by water, laddie."

"Sea water?"

"That's the one thing we'll not run out of."

"Right," I said.

"And make sure you hang on tightly when you lower the bucket over the side," he called after me.

So that's why it had such a long rope attached. Back on deck, I balanced my hips against the narrow ledge along the top of the bulwark, held on with one hand, wound the rope around my other hand, leaned over and lowered the bucket over the side. As it hit the sea, the rope tightened around my hand, crushing my fingers and dragging my arm down. I began to slither across the bulwark. The rope had pulled too tight to shake free. I clung to the ship with one hand, my bucket arm about to pull out of its socket.

"Help," I yelled. "HEEEELP."

Hands grabbed my legs and pulled me back onto the deck. One sailor unwound the rope from my crushed hand while another pulled up the bucket. Water sloshed out as it swung to and fro.

"For mercy's sake," cried the captain. "You promised me you wouldn't cause any more trouble."

"I was trying to wash my clothes, sir."

The captain grimaced as he took in the state of my trousers and the inch of water left in the bucket.

"Pickersgill," he snapped. "Show Mr. Tremayne how to belay a bucket without drowning." And off he strode.

Like everyone else, Pickersgill was taller than me but barely a year or so older from the look of him. He showed me how to slot a stout wooden peg into the ship's side, and wrap the bucket rope around the peg.

"*Now* lower the bucket," he said.

It was much easier, even with my bruised hand.

* * *

"Took you long enough," was all the thanks I got when I handed father the rinsed jug. He snatched it and made an odd noise in his throat. I grabbed my bundle of possessions and went to the head to change my clothes and wash. Back on deck it was windier than ever and we were flying smaller sails. I washed my shirt and trousers in the shelter of the wheelhouse.

Leaning into the wind with my head down, wet clothes clutched against my chest, I rounded the animal pens and smacked into the man who'd told me about stowaways. He grabbed me as the ship pitched down a particularly deep wave and somehow we managed to stay on our feet.

"What the devil are you doing with my bucket?" he asked.

"I only borrowed it."

"It's for cleaning out the animal pens. It stays here." He glared at me.

"Are these your pigs, sir?"

"Temporarily. The sooner I get rid of them the better, especially that ornery beast." He nodded at the boar. "He'd have been butchered long ago if it wasn't for the fact that he sires large litters of prize-winning piglets."

I had a glimmer of an idea. "I could look after them for you," I said. "I kept pigs back home."

"Why would *you* want to look after them?"

"To earn some money."

He looked at the boar's mean piggy eyes then back at me and told me what he wanted done. We agreed on a price, introduced ourselves, and shook hands on the deal.

"Take good care of them," said Mr. Hughes, "or the deal's off."

"I will, I promise."

"And watch out for that boar, he's a sneaky beast."

* * *

I hung my wet clothes over chairs in a corner of the deserted dining room and hoped no one would notice them dripping onto the floor. My cheeks burned from the wind and I rubbed my hands together to warm them up. Where was everyone? They couldn't all be sick in bed. I moved closer to the doorway and sat down. I'd never had nothing to do before.

I pulled my slate and chalk out of my bundle and tried to write the letter 'f.' The ship hit a trough and the chalk squealed across the slate. I tried again but the ship rolled over the top of a wave and the chalk took off again with a life of its own. I stared at the scribble on the slate. If I wanted to work in the mine's office I'd have to do better than that. My only other idea so far was to add to my pig money so I could pay the mining company for my voyage and find work elsewhere.

"What are you doing?" asked Hanna, coming up behind me.

Startled, I sprang to my feet and turned my slate over. "I'm thinking, Miss Spargo."

Hanna turned my slate face up and frowned at my smudged and jerky letters.

"I could do better than this with my left hand"

"So could I," I shot back.

"Then why don't you?"

"Because the vicar's nephew said he'd tie my left hand behind my back if he caught me writing with it again."

"That's ridiculous. Use whichever hand you want. Shall I help you?"

I hesitated, torn between the humiliation of being taught by a girl who was possibly younger than I was, and wanting to learn.

"I could help you read, too," said Hanna.

Without waiting for an answer, she sat beside me, rubbed my slate clean, and wrote *furl five sails* in small neat letters along the top. I tried to copy them but, even though it felt more natural to use my left hand, the chalk zigged and zagged.

"It's hard with the ship plunging up and down," I said.

"You'll get used to it. We'll do this every afternoon, and tomorrow I'll bring something for us to read." She stood up. "Your jersey matches your eyes you know."

She hesitated, blushed, then scurried off. I felt as though she'd punched me in the stomach. Mother had knitted my jersey for Christmas. She'd knitted Henry one too.

"The green matches our Trelawney eyes," she'd said, her knitting needles bobbing over the bulge that should have been another brother.

Henry wore his jersey on Christmas day but I couldn't put mine on. I took it to the pigsty and cried until it was soggy. Now, I brought a sleeve up to my nose and caught a lingering trace of the lavender Mother placed amongst her clothes. I closed my eyes and breathed it in. "I'm trying," I whispered to her. "I didn't know it would be so hard."

Chapter 15

Father was asleep when I looked in on him after supper and I was relieved to find our jug was still clean. His bones had grown more prominent over the months since Mother died. If he didn't start eating again soon there wouldn't be anything left of him. Someone had cleaned the floor but the sour smell lingered and I debated whether to spend the night in the locker again. There were no drafts in steerage though. No flapping sails, thrumming ropes, or wailing wind either. I lay on my bunk and pulled my blanket over my face to cut out the smell.

* * *

Next thing I knew, some of the miners were getting up for breakfast. I asked Father if he'd like some.

"No," he said, sitting up. "I do have a monstrous thirst though. Fetch me a mug of water, will you?"

While he sipped it, I sat on my bunk and prodded my feet. It was hard to see much in the gloom but the raw spots didn't hurt when I pressed them.

"Miss Spargo's going to help me with my reading and writing," I said.

"Who's Miss Spargo?"

"The captain's daughter."

"I'm glad you're doing something useful," said Father.

The ship pitched over an extra large wave. Father grabbed the jug, vomited up the water then groaned and lay back. There was nothing I could do. I left him to his misery.

After two helpings of porridge, I fed and watered the pigs. I'd just finished when I heard a clank and turned to see Hanna with a bowl of chicken feed.

"Miss Spargo." I nodded in greeting. "You look after the chickens?" I asked, as if that wasn't obvious.

"The captain likes to keep everyone busy. He says a busy ship is a happy ship."

Hanna slipped into the hen coop.

"Why do you call your father the captain?" I asked.

"Because he *is* the captain." Hanna looked at me as though this was a really stupid question.

As I tried to think of something more intelligent to say, the ship's bell rang once. Since it obviously wasn't one o'clock this brought another possibly stupid question to mind. I wouldn't have asked it, but I was used to having order to my days. Aboard the Fortuna I didn't know what time it was, what day it was or even where I was. I decided to go for it.

"Why did the ship's bell just ring?"

"To mark the forenoon watch."

I must have looked clueless because Hanna glanced at me then went on to explain.

"The crew is divided into two watches and each one takes turns at being on duty."

She looked at me again so I nodded.

"All watches last four hours except for the dog watches, which are split so the men can all eat around six o'clock in the evening, and so they work alternate times each day. The middle watch begins at midnight, while the first watch is actually the final watch of the night. Got that?"

"Sort of."

There was more.

"The bell rings off the half hours of each watch, beginning with one ring at the first half hour and ending with eight rings at the end of the watch."

Hanna looked at me expectantly.

"So … the bell that just rang was marking the first half hour of a watch?"

"Exactly. The Forenoon watch begins at eight o'clock in the morning so when the bell rang it was half past eight. At nine o'clock the bell will ring twice and so on. It's really very simple."

Simple for her. Luckily Hanna changed the subject as she poured the feed into a pan.

"I hate the way chickens peck at my feet."

"Pigs are all right though."

"If they don't trample you trying to get their heads in the swill bucket. And thank goodness I don't have to clean him out." Hanna nodded towards the boar.

"That's my job."

"How come?"

"I need something to do. I might as well earn some money."

"You know they're only going as far as Canada?" Hanna began sorting through the nesting hay in the coop.

"Do you know how much the mining company paid for my passage?"

"The captain would know. Would you like me to ask him?

"Please. How long will we stop in Canada?"

"However long it takes to clear customs and quarantine, change cargo, and re-provision."

"Will we have time to go ashore?"

And perhaps earn more money.

"If you can convince the captain you'll be back on time."

It was time to change the subject again.

"Have you always sailed with your father?"

"Since I was seven. Before that I lived with my mother in Portsmouth but she died." Hanna found an egg. "They don't lay much when the weather's rough," she said.

"I'm sorry about your mother. Mine died just before Christmas."

"There's no need to be sorry. I can only remember bits and pieces. Like a dress mother made me for my fifth birthday. And I remember things about our house, and people coming for the funeral all dressed in black. But I couldn't tell you what my mother looked like. I wish I could but I've forgotten."

"Then you're lucky. I wish I could forget so I didn't wake up every morning missing her."

"I don't feel lucky. Aunt Harriet wants me to go and live with her."

"Why?"

"*She says* a ship is no place for a young woman dressed in trousers like a boy. Instead of running wild I should be learning things to help me make a good marriage. She doesn't care what *I* want."

I knew what that was like.

"Aunt Harriet's a seamstress. She gets so excited about different stitches and fancy cloth. I told her I'd die of boredom if I had to sit and sew all day. *She* said I couldn't know that until I'd tried it."

"I know I can't work down the mines but Father won't listen."

"Why do grownups always think they know best," said Hanna. It wasn't a question.

"Will your father *make* you live with your aunt if you don't want to?"

Hanna sighed and gave up on her egg hunt. "I didn't think so, but lately he's been saying that *perhaps* his sister is right and I *will* be turning fourteen in July and we *must* think about it."

That made Hanna nine months younger than me. She sighed again, then looked at the egg in her bowl.

"I'll take this to Mac. Come and say hello."

I had a feeling I'd already met Mac but I followed Hanna into the kitchen, or the galley as she called it, and Hanna introduced us.

"Aye, the laddie worried about washing," Mac said, as we shook hands.

"And that," said Hanna, pointing to a striped cat asleep on a barrel, "is Tiger but don't try to pet him. He'll scratch you."

"Doesn't Tiger like strangers?"

"Tiger does not like anyone," said Mac, who was chopping a mound of turnips. His missing left hand didn't slow him down at all.

"Then why do you keep him?"

"He catches the rats," said Mac. "They sneak aboard *this* ship and soon find they've made a god-awful mistake."

"Not just rats," said Hanna. "Tiger catches cockroaches, spiders, mice. He's even caught a snake or two."

"Make yourselves useful," said Mac, gesturing towards two buckets piled with potatoes and carrots.

"You can peel the potatoes," said Hanna, handing me a knife. "I'll start on the carrots."

"Why do people get seasick?" I asked.

"If I knew the answer to that I'd be a rich man." Mac swept the last of the chopped turnips into a large pan wedged between his stomach and the counter.

"Only my father hasn't kept any food down since he came on board."

"Don't you worry, laddie. Many people get seasick first time on a ship. It'll clear up in a few days."

Mac hacked chunks of beef from a carcass as he told me about pirates who'd sheltered in Soper's Hole, a natural harbour on the largest of the Virgin Islands.

"There was Gustav Wilmerding," said Mac. "His musicians played music while he captured other ships and rang bells when he arrived home with stolen bounty. He lived on Tortola."

"Were the islanders scared of him?"

"Och, they kept away from the lewd parties and strange goings on. But even scarier was Edward Teach. You know what they called him?"

I shook my head.

"Blackbeard."

"Because of his beard?"

"It was nae ordinary beard. It covered his entire face, hung down his chest and gave off a smoky haze like the devil himself."

"What did he do?" "Starved his wives. Marooned his own men."

"Is he still alive?"

"Nae laddie. When he tried to board his final ship, a high-lander sliced off Blackbeard's head with his broadsword and slung it off his bowsprit as a warning to others. They threw his body into the sea. 'Tis said it swam several times around the ship before it sank."

"Are *we* likely to meet pirates?"

"Och, Blackbeard and Wilmerding lived long ago."

Chapter 16

The wind no longer threatened to tear the shirt from my back as I looked for the doctor. He was in a heated discussion with Captain Spargo. As I waited, the sailors began to raise extra sails and one of the men broke into song.

"I'm a deep water sailor just in from Hong Kong."

The others hauled on the ropes in time to their chorus, "To my way haye, blow the man down."

"If you give me some grog, I'll sing you a song," sang the leader.

"Give me some time to blow the man down," responded the men.

They were surprisingly tuneful and by the time the captain and doctor broke up their discussion, I was humming along. I ran to catch up to the doctor.

"Please sir?" I tugged at his sleeve.

"Master Tremayne. How are your feet?"

"They're healing, but my father needs help."

"What's wrong with him?"

He's seasick."

"He'll get over it in another day or two. Bring him up on deck. A bit of fresh air should help."

I went below and asked Father if he'd take a walk on deck with me. Perhaps the breeze would put some colour into his ashen cheeks.

"I don't feel up to it," he said.

"But it's stuffy down here. You could sit in the saloon for a while."

I was afraid his strangeness might return while he lay alone, staring into the gloom, but I couldn't persuade him so I went to meet Hanna for my first lesson.

The dining room and saloon were growing busier as other passengers gained their sea legs. Hanna brought two mugs of tea and some brown, shrivelled things she called dates to a quiet corner. The dates didn't smell of anything much so I popped one into my mouth. It was sweet and chewy, much tastier than it looked.

"Watch out for the stone in the middle," she said, waving a magazine in the air. "We're going to read Charles Dickens. He's writing a serial about a boy named Oliver Twist. We can take turns to read out loud and, since you're eating, I'll begin."

I settled back, chewing on another date and enjoying the warmth of the tea mug in my hands. Hanna read slowly but surely, whereas I struggled through "par-i-sion-ers would re-bell-i-ous-ly a-ffix their sig-na-tures to a re-mon ... remon-strance."

"*What* is a remonstrance?" I asked

"A complaint," said Hanna,

"I suppose your father taught you to read," I said, needing a break.

"And a couple of the ship's doctors. Oh, and one voyage we had a scientist aboard. He taught me all sorts of things." Hanna's cheeks dimpled when she smiled.

We stopped reading when the men who ran the workhouse offered Oliver Twist for sale to anyone who would apprentice him to a trade. It seemed Oliver and I had something in common.

* * *

The wind changed direction later that evening and I woke in the night to hear Father retching.

"I only took a sip of water," he whispered between heaves. "I'm so thirsty."

By the time Father's stomach had stopped trying to turn itself inside out, I was wide awake. Had the police arrested Jory and Dr. Basset? Did they even know where Dr. Basset was?

The price we paid for our cosy berth out of wind and spray was that very little fresh air found its way into steerage. It reeked of stale sweat and farts. Now that everyone had their bearings, we no longer kept the lanterns lit at night. I waved a hand in front of my eyes but couldn't see it. So why didn't I feel the panic that overwhelmed me in the darkness of the mine? Was it the earthy smell that made my heart race and my head spin? And why was I so ashamed I couldn't tell anyone? How was I going to tell Father what really happened to Henry?

* * *

Mindful of the doctor's instructions, I was scooting around one of the pig pens with my trouser legs rolled up and my left foot inside a metal pan, borrowed from Mac, to keep it out of the filth. Hanna leaned over the half-gate to the pen.

"What *are* you doing?" she asked.

"Seeing to the pigs." I casually lifted my foot out of the pan hoping Hanna wouldn't notice.

"How did you get such impressive bruises?"

My shins and most of my left foot were a purplish-black.

"I … slipped on some rocks." Not wanting to revisit my embarrassing arrival aboard, I changed the subject.

"Now we can't see land, how does the captain know which direction to sail?"

"He takes measurements and marks where we are on his charts."

"What does he measure?"

"The height of the sun above the horizon."

"But there isn't any sun today."

Hanna had a stalk of hay sticking out of her hair.

"Why don't you ask the captain," she said.

I shook my head. "That's not a good idea."

"Why not. He loves to talk about his ship."

"I don't think he wants to talk to *me*." Hanna's eyes twinkled again.

"He was angry when you held up our departure. He would have left without you if Mr. Reddiman hadn't had the new chronometer in the ship's boat at the dock. But he's not one to hold a grudge."

"What's a crow nometer?"

Hanna opened the gate, grabbed my arm, and pulled me out of the pen with surprising strength. Luckily I'd pretty much finished with the pigs because next thing I knew we were standing in the doorway to the wheelhouse. At least, Hanna was. I was trying to hide behind her. A feat made easier by her extra height.

"Are you busy?" she asked of someone inside.

"I'm never too busy for you, my dear," said a voice I recognized as the captain's.

"Mr. Tremayne wants to know how you navigate the ship." Hanna stepped aside.

"Does he now." The captain examined my face, then nodded at some private thought.

"I suppose if we keep you busy, you'll have less time to cause trouble. Of course I can't possibly impart a lifetime of learning in one morning, but we can make a start if you like?"

I nodded, then managed to get out the words, "Yes, sir."

"Come in."

Hanna waved goodbye.

"Navigation," the captain continued, "is all about accurate measurement, reliable observation and a generous sprinkling of intuition. My helmsman is steering by our compass. There was a time when men were afraid to use a compass in case people thought they were magicians under the influence of an infernal spirit. Imagine that! Do you believe in magic, Irwyn?"

I searched the captain's face for clues to the answer.

"N-n-no sir?"

"Neither do I, but a lot of sailors do and when you are in charge of a ship you have to understand how your crew members' minds work."

"But why would they think a compass was magic, sir?"

And so began my first lesson in navigation. The captain explained the ship's compass to me, unrolled charts and filled my head with facts and stories. By the time he dismissed me, saying he needed peace and quiet while he recorded the morning's progress, my head was reeling.

Later, when I met with Hanna in the saloon, she handed me a quill, some ink, and a book.

"These are for you," she said.

I flipped through the book.

"There's nothing in it."

"It's a diary. You write in it."

Wishing just once I could think of something funny or clever to say to Hanna, I mumbled my thanks and we read how Oliver Twist narrowly escaped being apprenticed to a chimney sweep, and being sent to sea. He was instead apprenticed to an undertaker but I think he'd have been better off at sea.

Chapter 17

By the end of our first week, the only person still seasick was Father. His sunken cheeks were grey. After breakfast, I went to find the doctor.

"They're healing nicely," he said, looking at my scabs and yellowish-green bruises before I could ask him to help my father.

"He hasn't eaten since he came on board, sir. He looks awful."

"Fresh air didn't help?"

"He wouldn't leave his bed, sir."

The doctor sighed. "He can hardly expect me to help if he doesn't do what I say." A short while later, we were up on deck with Father propped between us.

"See, it's much calmer here amidships," said the doctor. "Now keep your eyes on the horizon and take some deep breaths."

The sea was dark blue and the swell and chop had flattened somewhat. A cry went up as Father gripped the side of the ship.

"Whale off the port bow."

A vast grey back curved above the water then sank again. The passengers on deck rushed to the side to look. I peered into the waves hoping the whale would breach again.

"That reminds me of the time …" The doctor stopped mid-sentence as Father bent over the bulwark and retched. He had nothing to bring up and began to shiver.

"Take me back to bed," he said, as he wiped a string of slime from his chin.

"It's too stuffy down there," said the doctor.

We found Father a seat in the saloon.

"There," said the doctor. "Now your son's going to fetch you a blanket and ask Mac to make some ginger tea. It's very calming and you'll soon feel better." Despite his confident words, he placed a bowl in Father's lap before he left.

The shrivelled, brown, ginger root was fibrous and bled a clear liquid when I cut into it. I put a sliver in my mouth and spat it out as it burned my tongue. Hopefully, the tea would taste better. Mac told me to wrap small chunks in a piece of cloth and steep them in boiling water. I washed breakfast dishes while I waited. When I took the tea back to Father, he wrapped his hands around the warm mug. I draped his blanket across his shoulders like a shawl and went to see to the pigs.

Heeding Mr. Hughes' warning, I'd been filling the boar's food and water troughs from outside his pen but needed to go inside to clean it. I deliberated whether to enter with his swill bucket and hope it would distract him or leave my hands free for a quick escape. I decided upon the latter. The boar glared at me as I opened his gate just enough to sidle around it. His head went down and he lunged towards me. I slid back and pulled the gate shut as he slammed into it. I gave the matter more thought.

Lengths of old rope were never thrown away but spliced together to make useful longer pieces. Frayed bits and short scraps were untwisted and stuffed into hull seams or cracks. I found a piece that was several feet long, tied it around the base of the foremast and pulled on it to make sure it wasn't rotten. It held. I untied it, took it over to the boar's pen, poured his swill into his trough and leaned over the gate, talking to him. As he rooted through the swill, I tied the rope to his collar and secured the other end so he could only move his head a few inches in either direction. He didn't notice until I vaulted over his gate and began to sweep out his waste. Then he tugged at the rope, squealing loud enough to wake the dead, but couldn't reach me. I kept well clear of his sharp hooves and teeth as I swept. I sluiced the floor with seawater, then leaned from outside the gate and untied him. He glared at me for a moment or two, grunted, then turned back to his trough. Glad that duty was over, I stopped to watch the piglets next door. The one I thought of as Charley, because he was always pleased to see me, trotted over and I wished I had a treat for him. Did the real Charley miss me? And was it only seven days since we'd left our cottage?

I made my way to the saloon only to find Father's seat empty, his mug on the table still full of ginger tea. I rushed down to steerage to find him huddled in his bunk, sound asleep, the blanket still round his shoulders.

Wondering how I could make the stubborn fool obey the doctor, I stomped out on deck and tripped over a mound of canvas. I bashed my elbow as my knees slammed into the deck.

"Watch where you goin'," said a voice.

Beneath the canvas was the slender, dark-skinned sailor who'd taken me for a stowaway that first evening on board.

"Sorry," I choked out as, to my dismay, a tear rolled down my cheek. I turned my head away and struggled to my feet. The sailor grabbed my arm.

"Somethin's wrong," he said.

I nodded and swallowed hard. "I only came on this voyage because my Father begged me to and now he's doing his best to die of seasickness."

"Seasickness can make a person *wish* they were dead, but I never known it *kill* anyone," said the sailor.

Seated on an upside down wooden crate, he held a thick needle and was patching a sail that spilled down his legs onto the deck.

"He won't do what the doctor tells him."

The sailor fastened off the thread he'd been sewing then held out his right hand.

"Emile," he said. "Emile Labasilier."

"Irwyn Tremayne." I shook his hand and wondered what to say now that I'd blurted out my troubles.

Emile busied himself with his sail, then broke the silence.

"I know a man who wears bands round his wrists. He says they keep him from feelin' sick."

"Bands?"

"Right here." Emile circled one wrist with finger and thumb just below his wrist bone. "Reckon we could make some for your father if you like."

"Yes, please."

Emile went below. Behind us, foam bordered a lane of calm water that trailed dark blue the way we had come. Looking at the rough sea ahead I clasped my hands, bowed my head, and asked for help.

Emile returned with lengths of narrow cord. He showed me how to plait three of them then worked on a second set so we had two bands each the width of my thumb nail. We took them to Father who was now awake.

"They have to be tight," Emile explained, as Father held out his wrists. "But not so tight the blood can't flow."

"How long before he can eat?" I asked.

"When he done feelin' sick."

Emile left and I sat on my bunk and told father about the pigs on board and how I was reading Oliver Twist with Miss Spargo.

"Are the bands working yet?" I asked, after a while.

"I don't know," said Father.

"I could go and ask Mac for something to eat."

"Give them a while longer. Don't feel you have to sit here with me though. I'll be all right."

* * *

Pickersgill was a tall, gangly youth with that pinched look of people who never have enough to eat. Perhaps, like me, he had fallen foul of Mr. Reddiman and tried to avoid him, because he was never where he was needed and Mr. Reddiman was forever calling out "Pickersgiiiill." I came across him hidden in a corner behind the wheelhouse staring out to sea.

"Thanks for your help with the bucket," I said, as he looked up, startled.

The sleeves of Pickersgill's cotton shirt ended well short of his wrists and he never wore a jacket even in the coldest of winds.

"This is my first time on a sailing ship."

"Me too," he said. "I didn't think it would be like this."

"Like what?"

"So much to do. Always someone on at me. I'm so tired by the end of my watch but then I can't sleep.

"Why not?"

"My bunk's too short, and the ship pitches up and down, and the other men burp and fart and call out in their dreams."

"That doesn't seem to stop me from sleeping."

"You're lucky then." He was about to say something more when we heard his name being called. He rolled his eyes and ran off.

I would hardly say I was lucky. Sleep came easily but I dreamed of Father being taken to the asylum, and of Henry calling out for me from the bottom of a dark pit where I couldn't find him. I wouldn't be surprised if *I* called out in my sleep. I yelled a lot in my dreams.

At supper time I took Father a mug of Mac's fish stew. He sniffed it then took a tentative sip. I hoped the wrist bands were doing their job.

"I'll take this slowly," he said. "You go get your own supper."

I ate quickly then went to see if Father wanted more. He was slumped back in his bunk, the water jug on his lap. He looked up when he heard my approach.

"It wouldn't stay down."

He'd only swallowed a little of the broth. I took the mug back to the galley.

"Not working then" said Mac, when he saw my face.

I shook my head, too disappointed to speak.

"I have a suggestion," said Mac.

Chapter 18

"What the blazes is aqua puncture?" asked Father as Mac and I stood beside his bunk the next morning. He'd swung between being grumpy and being pitiful ever since we'd boarded the Fortuna. This morning he was definitely grumpy.

"I learned it from the Chinese," said Mac. "Your stomach is upset because your Qi or vital energy is blocked. I can use needles to unblock it."

"Needles?" Father turned even paler.

"Very fine needles," said Mac, rolling the letter 'r.' He untied a bundle of cloth held between his body and left stump to display a set of silver needles each barely thicker than a human hair. "You won't even feel them go in."

His reassurance was lost on Father who took one look at the needles and fainted clean away.

"Go ahead," I said. "Stick them in before he comes round."

"Roll up his trouser leg, high as you can," Mac instructed. "Now take a pinch of flesh right there," Mac pointed to the side of Father's thigh. "That's it."

He inserted the first needle. It was flexible and rounded but sharp at the tip so it slid in easily. Mac soon had a neat row of needles protruding down Father's leg. I didn't see how these would open up channels of vital energy but Mac seemed to know what he was doing.

"They don't bleed much," I said, too intent on what we were doing to notice that Father was coming round.

"What don't bleed?" asked Father. He lifted his head, took one glance at his leg and fainted again.

"Poor bugger," said Mac. "I don't think he likes needles."

By the time Father came round again, Mac had finished.

"Now you just lie there quietly for a wee while," Mac said, leaning in towards Father so he couldn't see that his leg looked like a gruesome human pincushion. It was hard to believe it didn't hurt but Mac had assured me that a dull ache was the worst Father would feel. I tried to think of a way to distract him and remembered something I'd overheard.

"People were talking about The Devil's Triangle at supper yesterday," I said.

"Och, aye?" said Mac.

"With its strange goings on."

"Strange indeed," said Mac. It didn't take much to get him talking. "Ships disappear. Men disappear. A slaver was found drifting with nothing but skeletons on board. A deserted barque was found with a meal still on the mess table and chairs kicked over as though the men had left in a hurry, or been in a fight. But there was no sign of her crew."

"What happened to them?"

"No one knows but The Triangle has deadly calms and vast strange-looking mats of weed float on the surface of the sea. I once met a sailor whose schooner had come across a derelict ship there. The captain put some of his ablest men on board and the two ships sailed for port. Two days later the captain noticed the derelict ship sailing erratically. He turned back and boarded her but found no sign of his men. They'd disappeared and no one ever saw them again."

"What's deadly about a calm sea?" asked Father.

"Without wind, a ship can only drift where the sea takes her. If she drifts for too long she runs out of food and water. Men can go without food for a while but to go without water is a terrible thing."

"Are we going there?" I asked.

"Nae laddie. The captain will steer well clear of The Triangle."

Father was all right until Mac began to remove the needles. When he slid the first one out, Father closed his eyes and I could see his Adam's apple going up and down as he swallowed repeatedly. At the fifth needle Father made a grab for the water jug and retched dryly.

"He told me it wouldn't hurt," I said, after Mac had taken his needles back to the galley.

"It didn't," said Father, "but the feel of needles sliding through flesh turned my stomach."

When the captain asked after Father, later that morning, I told him what had happened.

"Hmmm," he said. "There is one more thing we can try. It isn't very pleasant but it's been known to work."

"We'd best wait a bit," I said. "His muscles must be aching from the dry heaves."

"Well this will make him heave even more so we might as well get it over with. Go and ask Mac for a small piece of salt pork on a string."

"The idea," the captain told Father a short while later, "is that you swallow the salt pork with Irwyn holding onto the string so he can pull it back up your throat. He repeats this action until you're sick as a dog. When you've stopped being sick, you'll feel better."

I didn't point out Father had already been sick as a dog and it hadn't helped at all. He eyed the piece of fatty pork, his pale face taking on a green tinge.

"We'd better do this on deck," he said.

Father's jaunty walking stride had given way to an old man's shamble since we'd come aboard. He tottered to the ship's side, where clean up would be easy, and held on. I dangled the piece of pork in front of his mouth. Father closed his lips around it and tried to swallow. He began retching before it was even half way down his throat and I thought he was going to choke. I yanked on the string, threw the pork overboard, then fetched an upturned crate for Father. When seawater had washed away the last strings of stomach slime, I helped him back to his bunk then went to make another mug of ginger tea. When I tried to give it to Father he wouldn't take it.

"No more remedies," he said. "Just leave me be."

"But you have to drink."

He closed his eyes.

"You have to drink and you have to eat," I shouted. "Don't think you're going to die on this ship and leave me to work down the mine. I hate mines. I only came because of a promise I made to Mother. And you promised things would be better but they stink."

Aware of Mother's locket around my neck, I wiped a sleeve across my eyes and blundered out to the head. It was the only place I could be alone. "I'm trying," I said, pressing the warm locket against my skin. "I really am trying."

In the saloon that afternoon, I opened my diary and began to write. Painstakingly formed letters quickly gave way to an outpouring that gushed like blood from a fatal wound. When the words dried up, I stabbed a final full stop that made a hole in the page. I looked up to find Hanna watching me with a concerned expression. Sure she must be able to read my painful thoughts, I turned back to my barely legible scrawl splattered with ink blots.

"Want to talk about it?" asked Hanna

I shook my head and stood up so quickly my chair fell backwards with a thunk. I strode to the doctor's cabin, banged on the door and opened it. The doctor looked up from something he was writing. I didn't wait for him to speak.

"He won't drink ginger tea. I've tried fresh air, wrist bands, aqua puncture, fish stew and salt pork and he's still sick as a dog. If you don't help us, he's going to die."

The doctor rubbed his hands up and down his face as though washing it.

"Sit down." He gestured towards a chest and I sat. "Fish stew and salt pork are too rich for someone who hasn't eaten for over a week. Forget the sailors' remedies. As long as he's drinking …"

"But he's not," I burst in. "He can't even keep water down."

The doctor sighed. "Let's go and see Mac."

In the galley, we warmed up some porridge left over from breakfast and stirred in a spoonful of treacle.

"Has he had stomach problems before?" asked the doctor, as I carried the porridge down to steerage.

I shook my head. "He was fine until he stepped aboard the Fortuna." Which wasn't strictly true but I didn't think this had anything to do with his rocking and blank gaze that made people think he was crazy.

Father was lying on his bunk staring at the deck above his head.

"Now Mr. Tremayne, how are you feeling?"

The doctor felt Father's wrist, looked at his eyes, his tongue and then helped him sit up. "This," he said, taking the bowl of porridge from me, "will help you to feel better. Now, open wide."

I watched anxiously as the doctor spooned porridge into Father's mouth. At the fifth spoonful, Father raised a hand and shook his head.

"Excellent," said the doctor. "We'll soon have you back on your feet."

I prayed the doctor was right.

He brought more porridge after supper and by the following afternoon, I had a more encouraging entry for my diary.

Tuesday, April 10, 1838

Father has not vomited for over 24 hours. He ate half a bowl of porridge for breakfast, and another at midday. Three cheers for Mac's porridge!

I wrote slowly, concentrating on well-formed letters and when Hanna looked over my shoulder and said, "Good," I didn't know whether she meant my writing or Father's eating.

* * *

The doctor told me to feed Father four times a day.

"And make sure he drinks lots of water," he added, "or he's going to be terribly constipated."

"I've added a wee drop of brandy," said Mac, when I picked up Father's afternoon ration. "It's very soothing to the stomach."

Given Father's opinion on the evils of liquor I could only assume he hadn't guessed why his porridge had an unusual smell. Nor was I about to say anything because last night he'd slept soundly for the first time since we'd left Cornwall. Mac slowly increased his portions and a couple of days later re-introduced cups of ginger tea stirred with heaped spoonfuls of sugar. Father's skin lost its grey tinge and his cheeks began to fill out again. With Father firmly back in the land of the living and well out of Dr. Basset's clutches, I wished I could enjoy the voyage but Henry revisited me nightly in my dreams. And what was I going to do when we reached Virgin Gorda?

Chapter 19

Apart from tending Mr. Hughes' pigs, I'd come up short of finding ways to earn money to pay off my passage onboard ship, however my reading and writing were slowly improving and with three months to think up other ways to avoid working in the Virgin Gorda mine, I gave myself up to the rhythm of life aboard the Fortuna. Remembering my earlier concerns that I'd have nothing to do made me smile. I helped crew members when I could and Emile was teaching me to tie knots. He made me practice over and over again until I could tie each one with my eyes shut.

"Knowin' the right knot can save lives," he said, when I asked if he could show me something new. "Now, tie that bowline again usin' one hand."

The captain and Hanna introduced me to chess one calm evening. I picked up one of the game pieces.

"That's a knight," said Hanna.

"Is it stone?"

"Whale bone," said the captain. "When it's carved like that we call it scrimshaw."

I turned it around marvelling at the delicately carved design. Hanna and the captain explained their moves as they played but I couldn't concentrate and finally excused myself. I curled into my bunk and pulled my blanket up around my chin, glad of the chance to think.

Guilt over leaving Henry in the flooded mine still brought me awful dreams. I hated keeping it a secret from Father and, now that he was recovering, I had no excuse to keep it from him any longer. Even if he despised me for leaving Henry alone to drown, perhaps he would accept that I wasn't born to be a miner.

My chance came the next morning. Although Father was still only eating porridge, and pushed aside any tidbits that Mac added to tempt him with, he ate with everyone else in the saloon. I'd woken late and by the time we'd finished eating, everyone else had gone. I pulled my chair closer to his.

"Father?"

"Yes Wyn?"

"There's ... something I have to tell you."

To my dismay, two of the miner's wives appeared. They nodded towards us with a "Mornin'", and settled themselves, one with her knitting and the other with a shirt she was mending.

"Go on then," said Father.

I didn't want witnesses spreading the latest gossip about me but Father was looking at me expectantly.

"I'm ... so glad you're eating again."

"*You're* glad? I thought the only way I was going to leave this ship was sewn into a shroud."

I suppressed a sigh. It was impossible to have a private conversation on the ship. I'd have to wait until we called in at Quebec.

* * *

One evening, we were gathered in the saloon where one of the miners was fiddling a toe-tapping tune when Hanna attracted my attention from the doorway and mimed that we should go outside. She led me up to the forecastle deck and pointed over the side of the ship.

With the moon dulled by cloud the sea looked like ink but the spray from the Fortuna's bow was full of pinpricks of light that danced over the water. Their flashes came and went so quickly I would have thought I was imagining them if they hadn't lit up over and over again. I recalled stories of mischievous and unsociable Cornish piskies who could appear like cottage lights and entice unwary travellers into bogs.

"Where are the lights coming from?" I whispered.

"Tiny creatures in the water," said Hanna.

Then perhaps they were piskies after all. From piskies my mind drifted to knockers and, inevitably, Henry. What would Hanna think if I told her I'd killed my brother?

"Your father's looking better," she said.

"He's eating, thank goodness, but he needs to gain weight. He gets tired doing nothing."

"What will you do at the mine?"

"Anything but work underground."

"You're lucky."

"Lucky? Me?" I thought of her father never being too busy for her and, for a moment, I wondered if Hanna was teasing but her expression was serious.

"Yes. You're a boy. You can be anything you want. You could be captain of this ship. I could never do that, no matter how much I know about sailing."

"But you don't need to work." "Why not?" "You'll find a husband."

"To cook and clean for?" She glared at me.

"Well, yes."

"And what if I don't want to be stuck at home cooking and cleaning? There has to be more to life than cooking stew and sewing buttonholes. I thought you, Master Tremayne, of all people, would understand."

Hanna turned and ran off

"I'm not lucky," I shouted into the wind.

Chapter 20

We began to run into fog patches and on the third of May we reached the Grand Banks of Newfoundland. Seabirds wheeled and plunged at great speed as they dived for fish. Hanna joined me as I watched their antics.

"Why are they attacking each other?" I shouted, over the squawking and screeching.

"Arctic skua are the pirates of the air. They'd rather steal food from other birds than catch their own."

As she spoke, a bird with a fish in its beak zoomed past our heads. A skua was right on its tail, dipping and pecking. The smaller bird let out a cry of dismay and dropped its fish. The skua dived and caught it.

Mr. Reddiman asked for volunteers to take turns as extra lookouts to watch for icebergs. I'd been keeping out of his way but perhaps this would get me back into his good books. I stepped forward.

"Not you, Tremayne," he said, loud enough for everyone to hear. "I need responsible people I can trust."

I bit back a retort and slipped away, glad I'd never have to work for Mr. Reddiman. The captain might not hold a grudge but his first mate obviously did.

The fog grew so thick we could scarcely see the length of the ship. Extra men stayed on lookout while another blew the fog horn as a signal to other ships. The mate ordered soundings taken. We hove to and bobbed about on the waves while the leadsman hoisted a heavy lead weight over the side then let out the attached line marked off in fathoms. When the lead hit bottom, the leadsman called out, "Fifty fathoms." Reassured that we weren't about to run aground, Mr. Reddiman shouted orders to resume our course.

I was glad of my thick woollen jersey and when Hanna came on deck she complained of the cold. We could hear whales blowing all around us and peered through shifting curtains of fog hoping to see them. We glimpsed a few grey humps and a fin.

* * *

By morning the fog had been replaced by leaden clouds and it began to snow. Winter storms back home sometimes brought icy snow pellets that stung bare skin. These snowflakes fell like feathers that gathered in the folds of my clothing. I opened my mouth and let them melt on my tongue. They piled up on the deck and I scooped up a handful, shaped them into a ball and, catching sight of Hanna, gently lobbed it at her. It caught her on the shoulder and she turned, saw me, and threw one back. The fight was on, until Mr. Reddiman passed by. Still smarting from yesterday's snub, I fired off a snowball that thwacked against his ear. He turned to glare at me.

"Tremayne, you son of a ... " He caught sight of Hanna and his cheeks flushed bright red.

I should have apologized before he stomped off but the words stuck in my throat.

The wind picked up until the snow blew horizontal and dead against us. Progress was slow and choppy. The sailors bundled up in extra jackets and hats. Tiger, who usually made himself scarce, moved into the galley and wouldn't leave.

* * *

The gale eventually eased and when the sun appeared early one morning, the Fortuna looked like a sparkling ghost ship with her rigging coated in snow and ice. I tried to persuade Father to take a look but he said it was too cold. By the time we passed Cape Breton Island, there were other ships in sight. Four days later, a schooner came alongside just before supper and dropped off a pilot to guide us the rest of the way up the St. Lawrence River.

Thinking the sight of farms and woodlands along the shoreline would cheer up Father, I thought I'd take him on deck before we went to eat. He was in his bunk and refused to get out.

"I ache all over," he said.

"But you've got to eat."

"I can't. My teeth hurt."

I raced back to the dining room where the doctor was eating.

"Something's wrong with Father," I panted. "He won't get out of his bunk."

"Another fifteen minutes won't make much difference. Eat your supper. We'll go and see him when we've both finished."

I have no idea what I ate.

Chapter 21

"Scurvy," announced the doctor, after examining Father.

"What's scurvy?" I asked.

"It's what you get when you won't eat anything but porridge."

He bent down so he could look Father in the face.

"If you continue on like this you're going to die. Now I'm going to see what Mac has to counteract this and whatever it is, you will eat it. Do you understand?"

My father nodded and the doctor strode off. I hurried after him.

"Why didn't you tell Father this before? You knew he was only eating porridge."

"It doesn't usually appear this quickly."

I followed him to the galley where, for once, there was no sign of Tiger.

"'The boy's father is developing scurvy.'"

"Already?" said Mac. "I've tried adding a few currants or some small pieces of meat to his porridge but he will nae eat them."

"And now his gums are bleeding so he'll find it hard to chew. Have you got something soft he can have?"

"Mashed turnip. There's a few left in the bottom of the barrel."

"Good. Mix some into his porridge." The doctor turned to me. "And make sure he eats it. If he looks ill when the doctor from Grosse Isle makes his inspection, we'll all be stuck in quarantine."

I made Father eat every last blob of porridge-turnip mash then took the bowl back to the galley.

"Could Father really die from scurvy?"

Mac nodded towards a mound of dirty dishes before answering. I lifted half a dozen bowls into the tub of sea water Mac had waiting and began to scrub.

"Aye, he could, but it happens slowly so we've time to get him right."

"What if he can't keep the turnips down?"

"Then we'll try something else. And we'll soon be in Quebec. A day or two on shore will help put his stomach to rights. Once he's eating properly, he'll be fine."

It was late when I left the galley and Father was asleep. I turned to my bunk ready to fall into bed and froze. Tiger was eating something bloody and disgusting. Probably a rat he'd caught but why did he have to eat it on my bunk? Torn between wanting to see and not wanting to see, I moved my lantern closer. Unable to believe my eyes, I bent down for a better look.

Tiger wasn't eating, he was licking a newborn kitten clean. But where had Tiger found a kitten? I had my answer a few minutes later when a second clump of bedraggled fur began to emerge from Tiger's straining backside. I watched as bit by bit he pushed the kitten out. I didn't dare touch it, although Tiger seemed too preoccupied to hiss and snarl his usual greeting. Or perhaps he was too tired. He pushed a third kitten into the world five or ten minutes later. I must have fallen asleep while waiting to see if there were any more.

* * *

I was lying on the floor when I woke in the morning, cold and cramped. Pins and needles stabbed my right foot. The kittens must have been a dream. They made an odd but welcome change from dreaming about searching for Henry in suffocating mines. Then I noticed the brown stain drying on my blanket. My first thought was to tell Hanna.

"You watched two kittens being born and didn't come and get me?"

"It was late and I was tired and totally flummoxed." And even if I'd known which was her cabin, I could hardly have banged on her door at that time of night. "Did you know Tiger was a girl?"

"Of course not. He never let us get close enough to find out. He, I mean she, certainly acted like an old tom cat, yowling and spitting at everyone."

"Let's go and tell Mac. He'll be surprised."

But he wasn't.

"You knew," said Hanna.

"Nae lass." Mac shook his head. "I almost poured tea leaves into the porridge when Tiger strolled into the galley this morning with a kitten dangling from his mouth."

Mac gestured at a crate tucked near the warm stove and as much out of the way as possible. I peered inside. Snuggled into a soft piece of cloth lay Tiger and three kittens all sound asleep.

Hanna knelt by the crate and made ooohing and aaahing noises. I mashed some boiled turnip and mixed it into Father's porridge. I was about to take it to him when I heard the rattling and clanking of the anchor.

"Are we there?"

"Nae laddie, the fog's back. It's as thick as my granny's gooseberry jam out there and what with all the islands and rocks and the other ships heading for Grosse Isle, it's too dangerous to proceed."

I told Father about having to anchor because of the fog, Tiger's kittens, and anything else I could think of to distract him as he ate the turnip-laced porridge.

* * *

When we finished reading Oliver Twist in the saloon that afternoon, Hanna said "that's all."

"It can't be."

Robbers had forced Oliver to break into a house and, after Oliver was shot, abandoned him in a ditch so they could escape pursuers.

"I've run out of instalments," said Hanna. "I bought this one just before we left Charlestown."

"How will we find out what happens?" I was developing a soft spot for Oliver.

Hanna shrugged. "I'll see if I can find more when we reach …" Someone screamed. We barely had time to exchange surprised looks before Andrew Hughes flung himself round the saloon door.

"Theboar'sout!" he gasped.

It took a moment for his words to register.

"Out?"

"As in charging around attacking people."

"How could he have got out?"

"Because you didn't shut him in properly."

"That's not true."

I took great care to see that his gate was latched and, for good measure, tied it snugly with my newly learned knots. There was no way the knots would undo themselves, but this wasn't the time to argue. Another scream reached us, louder this time, and I shot out of my chair and raced to the galley. There were a few shrivelled turnips left at the bottom of the barrel and I hesitated before grabbing two of them. It would mean two less for Father but I had to stop the boar before someone was hurt. I ran to his pen and snatched the rope I used when I cleaned it out. Hanna was right behind me and we exchanged glances. The fog had reduced our world to two paces in any direction so we stood, listening. We heard a shout and some scuffling.

"Forward," cried Hanna, pointing.

We made our way towards the bow then stopped as the boar's backside loomed out of the mist. He was intent on the foremast and a few more steps towards him showed Mr. Reddiman circling the base of the mast to keep it between him and the boar. I groaned. It would have to be Mr. Reddiman. I was trying to decide what to do when Hanna took off. She ran past the boar and slapped him on the backside as she passed. He turned to chase her. Hanna squeezed between the bulwark and one of the ship's boats. The boar, too fat to follow, squealed in frustration and butted upturned boat. Fortunately it was well secured.

I crept up on him, smacked the rope against his flank and raced to his pen. I ran inside, slammed the gate and dropped a turnip in front of it. He caught its scent and, as he bent to chew on his prize, I dropped the second turnip inside the pen, opened the gate and climbed onto it. He trotted towards the second turnip. I climbed over the gate, closed it behind him, and tied it securely. The boar's flanks heaved.

"Thanks," I said, as Hanna loomed up beside me.

"How did he get out?" she asked.

A good question! The gate catch was intact and there was nothing left of the knot I'd tied that morning. As I turned towards Hanna, I glimpsed Pickersgill's face melting into the fog behind her. "Someone opened the gate," I said.

I didn't hear what she said next because Mr. Hughes loomed out of the fog and began to yell.

"This is a valuable animal. I thought I'd made that clear."

To make matters worse, Mr. Reddiman appeared. "Tremayne!" he said. "I might have known you were involved."

"It wasn't my fault, sir. I tied the gate with two half hitches this morning. There's no way they came undone on their own."

"Then who untied them?" asked Mr. Hughes.

"Someone who doesn't like me."

Mr. Hughes snorted. "I shall be keeping a close eye on this beast. If he's sustained any injuries you will pay." And with this, Mr. Hughes and Mr. Reddiman stomped off in different directions.

"He looks all right to me," said Hanna, as a drop of blood plopped onto the floor of the boar's pen. I lay on the deck and looked up at his belly. Hanna joined me.

"There." I pointed to a scratch in his flank. "He must have caught it on something."

"Mac will know what to do," said Hanna. "Come on."

It was on the tip of my tongue to ask whether Mac might recommend a porridge and turnip poultice, however Hanna's faith in him as an expert on practically everything was well placed. Mac rummaged in a locker and produced a small pot of ointment. I took the lid off and sniffed.

"I bought it from a Chinese sailor. It works like a charm," said Mac. "Just rub a bit on the raw skin and it'll stop it from festering."

I had no idea how I was supposed to do this but the boar's romp around the deck must have tired him and when he'd snuffled up the last speck of turnip he settled down for a nap. For once I was in luck because he lay with the scratch exposed. I covered it with a glob of ointment and left it to soak in.

Sometime overnight the fog cleared and we resumed our way up river only to have the wind die on us. Would we ever reach Quebec?

Chapter 22

FRIDAY, MAY 18TH, 1838

I kept an anxious eye on both Father, who still lay aching in bed, and the boar, who seemed none the worse for his escapade. I didn't want to forfeit my fee for looking after him. We continued to make what progress we could by dropping anchor when the tide was going out, or ebbing as Hanna called it, and raising it to drift upriver with the incoming, or flood, tide.

When we finally reached the Grosse Isle quarantine ground two days later, we hoisted our signal and waited.

"Why can't they just let us off?" grumbled Father, his eyes glued to land we could almost touch. After five days on mashed turnip, his aches and pains were receding but he complained his gums still hurt.

"We'll soon be ashore," I said. "You'll feel better with solid food inside you."

Father didn't look convinced but the doctor took him for a walk on deck to "shake out the cobwebs."

Mid-morning a rowboat approached and the quarantine doctor was hoisted aboard. Father still looked pale and unsteady as we lined up but, as Mr. Beadle said in Oliver Twist, the wind was blowing "enough to cut one's ears off." Hopefully the doctor wouldn't linger over his inspection. Even Hanna was shivering as the doctor strode past the assembled passengers and crew, glancing at faces. He passed Father, stopped, then took two steps backwards.

"Have you had any fever?" the doctor asked.

"No, sir," said Father.

The doctor felt Father's forehead then told him to stick out his tongue. I couldn't imagine anyone would feel feverish after fifteen minutes in that wind. Nevertheless, I crossed my fingers and the ship was abnormally quiet as we waited for permission to proceed. When the quarantine doctor gave us the go-ahead, I could feel the communal relief.

We continued upriver, past a huge waterfall, and anchored in Quebec harbour but we still weren't allowed off the Fortuna.

"Why not?" I asked, as Hanna and I helped clean up the galley after supper.

"We have to be cleared by a customs inspector and a doctor," said Hanna.

"*Another* doctor?"

"They're afraid of cholera," said Mac. "They had a terrible epidemic six years ago brought by immigrants."

Father was sitting on an upturned crate staring at the Custom House, a long two-storey building of grey stone that rose above the mudflats and wharves along the waterfront.

"Best come to bed," I said. "We won't be allowed off tonight."

* * *

The doctor arrived at eight o'clock the next morning. When he was satisfied, the customs officer noted those passengers, like Mr. Hughes, who were staying in Canada. Then we moved onto one of the wharves and the crew tied the Fortuna into her berth.

Father and I went below to gather up our belongings and Father chatted with some of the other miners. Then the captain waylaid us on our way back to the deck and gave us directions to suitable lodgings.

"Mention my name and the owner will charge you a fair price," said Captain Spargo, looking at me. "And get some solid food into your father. As for you, sir," he put a hand on Father's shoulder, "you'll feel yourself again after a couple of days on solid ground."

"We'll be off then," said Father, obviously eager to put the captain's prediction to the test.

"Make sure you're back on board by noon on Wednesday," said the captain. "That's the day after tomorrow. If you're not here, we shall sail without you. Understand?"

"Yes, sir." I nodded, then caught up with Father. "I just have to collect my pig money."

"Hurry up then," said Father, looking cheerful for the first time in weeks.

I'd stayed out of Mr. Hughes' way since the boar's escape but the animal was none the worse for his adventure and Mac's ointment had done its job. I knocked on Mr. Hughes' cabin door. There was no answer. I knocked harder, then opened it. Mr. Hughes was not there. Nor were any of his personal belongings. I ran through the ship, dodging sailors and passengers but could find no sign of him. When I passed the animal pens I did a double take. The crates with the boar and Mr. Hughes' sows were gone. I caught sight of Mr. Reddiman.

"Have you seen Mr. Hughes?" I asked.

"He left as soon as we tied up."

"With his pigs?"

Mr. Reddiman nodded.

"But he hasn't paid me for looking after them," I gasped. "We had a deal."

"You think he's gonna pay you for letting his prize boar rampage?"

He must have got off while we were below, talking to the captain. Father was waiting by the gangplank. I grabbed his arm. "Come on," I said.

"What's wrong?" asked Father.

"Mr. Hughes left without paying me."

I started down the gangplank then stopped so suddenly that Father bumped into me. The Quebec waterfront below us was like an anthill under attack with people scurrying in all directions. I looked for Mr. Hughes.

"Are we going or not?" asked Father, back to his grumpy self.

I ran down the rest of the gangplank. Mr. Hughes would have needed help unloading the crates and he'd have had to find transportation for the pigs. He couldn't have gone far. I ran around the dock asking if anyone had seen a man with crates of pigs. Some people didn't understand what I was asking. Others shook their heads or simply ignored me, too busy with what they were doing. I should have asked for my money yesterday. I looked between buildings and snooped inside carts and warehouses until I finally had to admit that he'd gone.

"Damn."

I kicked a barrel that must have been full of something really heavy and limped back to Father. He was still where I'd left him, leaning against a post.

"I took him for a gentleman," I said. "We shook hands on the deal. I can't believe he left without paying me."

"People aren't always what they seem," said Father, as we set off towards the lodgings the captain had recommended. "And it's no good storming off, I can't walk that fast."

After weeks of eating hardly anything and doing nothing, Father had to rest every few minutes. We stopped to let him catch his breath and I found myself swaying as though I was still aboard the Fortuna's rolling decks. I'd have to kiss my pig money goodbye. So much for paying off my passage when we reached Virgin Gorda. Perhaps I could persuade Father to stay here. Surely we'd be able to find work in this busy place, if we could understand what people were saying. Few of them seemed to be speaking English. But then we wouldn't be any better than Mr. Hughes if we jumped ship and left the mining company to pay for our passage.

The landlady at the boarding house looked us over and paused at my left foot. It had long since healed but, with no boot to wear, I'd wrapped it in a rag for protection. Despite this she showed us to a room and, when we'd paid for two nights in advance, she offered us a cup of tea.

"Yes please," said Father, "but Wyn needs to buy new boots." He looked at me. "Go on. Don't worry about me."

"But what about lunch?" Both Mac and the doctor had told me to get as much fresh food into Father as possible while we were ashore.

In heavily accented English, the landlady said she could provide a bit of cold meat and some preserves.

"There you are," said Father. "I'll be all right."

Chapter 23

I followed our landlady's directions to a cordwainer who made workboots. As well as new boots, he had some second-hand ones. One pair was nearly new and only a bit too large. The cordwainer stuffed rags in the toes to make them fit.

Now that I could walk in comfort, my thoughts turned to Hanna. Her birthday was on July eleventh and I wanted to give her something. Then again, I thought I'd have my pig money. Could Mr. Hughes have simply forgotten about me in the excitement of coming into port? If only I'd asked where he was taking the pigs, I might have had some chance of finding him. I wandered past shop windows. I should conserve what money I had, even if it wasn't enough to pay off my passage. But my reading and writing were improving with Hanna's help. I owed her.

I glimpsed market stalls down a side road and made my way to a square where vendors were hawking their wares. The smell from a tray of steaming meat pies with golden pastry and savoury gravy seeping through slits in the top made my stomach gurgle but I could wait to eat until supper time. I distracted myself by examining the baskets and soaps and dried herbs for sale.

At one of the stalls, a woman was selling thread and lengths of cloth. A flash of bright red in a basket of remnants caught my eye. I put my old boot down for a moment and pulled out the piece of red cloth. It was so soft. I brushed it against my cheek and the stall owner said something I didn't understand. I unfolded the strip of cloth and thought of Hanna shivering on Fortuna's deck. If I hemmed the edges I could make a shawl. Just looking at the holly-berry red made me feel warmer.

"How much?" I asked. The woman held up three fingers.

"I'll need thread too," I said, pointing.

"Rouge?"

She picked up some red thread and I nodded.

"And a needle."

The woman frowned so I made sewing motions.

"Ah, oui." From a pocket, she took a scrap of cloth with a row of needles stuck along it, slid one out, and held it up for my approval. I nodded again. She rolled the thread into the cloth and pinned the needle in one corner. I handed her my money and strolled on to a stall of nuts and seeds. I stopped in front of baskets of dried black and red berries. One of the two men behind the stall pointed to the black ones.

"Blueberries," he said.

"And these?"

"Cranberries," he said. "'ere."

His sausage-like fingers were surprisingly nimble as he picked out one blueberry and one cranberry and offered them to me. I chewed them one at a time. The black one was sweet, the red one tart.

"Would they help someone with scurvy?" I asked

"But yes. They are good to take on a ship."

"Which ones are better?"

"The blueberries are sweeter but I think per'aps the cranberries 'ave more …" he searched for a word "…more goodness. I mix some of each for you?"

"How much do they cost?"

"You pay in sous, cents or pennies?

"Pennies."

"For an 'andful of each, twenty pennies."

Twenty pence was a lot. Even one handful would be ten pence. Disappointed, I turned away.

"What you pay?" the man asked.

I thought quickly.

"Your handful or mine?"

"Mine."

"Four pence for one handful."

"Six," said the man.

I hesitated. I probably wasn't going to have enough money to pay off my passage when we reached Virgin Gorda anyway. And I didn't want Father to have some nasty accident because he was weak and doddery. The second man whispered in the stall-owner's ear. The stall owner nodded.

"A special deal," he said. "If you will deliver something for my friend 'ere, I will pay you with an 'andful of berries."

"Done," I said.

The man piled the berries into a twist of paper. He had large hands. If I gave Father three or four berries a day, they would last a while. The second man pulled a package about the size of my diary from a pocket and handed it to me. He began to speak and the stall owner translated directions of where I was to take the package and who I was to give it to.

"Make sure you do exactly as 'ee says. 'Ee will know if you don't." He gave me the berries and I tucked them inside my old boot.

"Don't worry," I said, too pleased I didn't have to part with any more of my precious coins to worry about why he didn't want to deliver the package himself.

I set off past a church and followed directions the stall owner had made me repeat. The package was flexible but the string around the paper was tightly tied with too many knots for me to slip it off to see what was inside.

The neat shops and well-kept houses grew dingier until I was walking past shacks that held each other up. A skin-and-bones horse pulled an empty wagon, whipped on by a man dressed in rags.

"Need a ride?" he called.

I shook my head, slipped the package inside my jacket, and felt for my knife as I quickened my pace.

Chapter 24

The sign for The Red Dragon was layered with grime. If a seagull perched on top of it hadn't cried out as I passed, causing me to look up, I would have missed it. As my fist knocked against the door, it swung open. A woman with bright red lips and revealingly tight clothes turned and saw me.

"Yes?" She had a broken tooth.

"I have something for Monsieur Renard."

The woman smiled and gestured for me to follow her.

The inn smelled not of onions or ale or even sweaty bodies but of strangely sweet smoke. As we passed one room, I glimpsed a man lying on a bed smoking a long pipe. We came to a room with tables and chairs that was empty except for a man with a chewed-up ear behind the bar. He looked up as we approached.

"Are you Monsieur Renard?" I asked.

He nodded.

"I have a package for you."

He held out his hand, grunted as I handed him the package, and disappeared through a doorway.

"Come!"

The woman led me back through corridors into a small room. The strange smoke was making me light-headed. She pressed a hand down onto my shoulder and I fell into a soft armchair, clutching my spare boot in my lap.

"You like something, yes?"

I couldn't think straight.

"Wait," she said and walked away.

I knew I should leave. I willed my legs to stand up and leaned against the wall, then stumbled back into the hallway. My feet seemed to have a mind of their own as I half-shuffled and half-slid along the wall as quietly as I could. I reached a dead end and, cursing silently, slid and shuffled back the way I had come. I reached a junction and looked left then right, not recognizing either way. I shook my head to try to clear it and stumbled left. A man stood in a doorway talking to someone else in the room. The man looked out as I passed. I bit back a cry as I recognized bodysnatching Dr. Basset. Had he seen me? I hurried on. A puff of fresh air blew across my left cheek. I turned towards it. There was a door with grimy panes of glass at the end of the hallway. Fresh air wafted through a broken pane. I thudded a shoulder against the door and fell outside.

My steps were clumsy. I wanted to sit down but a voice in my head told me to keep walking. I forced myself to take deep breaths of damp, salty air. Where was I? Drunken singing came from an open doorway. More surefooted now, I began to run. Up ahead something sparkled in the sun. I jogged between two buildings and found wharves stretching out into the sea. I stopped to catch my breath, my thoughts too.

It couldn't possibly be Dr. Basset I'd seen in that doorway. The smoke had confused me. I'd seen a man of similar build. Someone with the same mousey hair. Tied back in the same way. From the same boney nose and a small scar along his jawbone ... I slumped against a wall. Why would Dr. Basset be in Quebec? Had he found out about my letter Charley had given to the constable? Could he still have Father committed on foreign soil? Was he following us? But he left Redruth long before us and we'd only just arrived. I wandered on trying to make sense of it all.

Several large ships were tied up in the distance. I made my way towards them and realized with relief that one was the Fortuna. I knew where I was now and retraced my earlier route to our lodgings. I tucked the roll of red cloth inside my jacket to avoid awkward questions from Father before climbing the stairs to our room.

"I'm hungry," Father said, when I walked in. "Let's find somewhere to eat."

He walked slowly and stopped outside the first place we came to, The Neptune Inn.

"Let's try in here," he suggested.

That was fine by me. If Dr. Basset *was* looking for us then the less time we spent outside, the less likely he was to find us. I didn't tell Father about him or The Red Dragon.

I tucked into my plate of cod, potatoes, and cabbage then finished off Father's when he said he was full. I had room left for the steamed sponge with a kind of runny treacle at the bottom. Back in our lodgings, I stretched out on my bed, unused to so much room. It was very quiet without the Fortuna's creakings and groanings. I lay for a long time wondering whether Dr. Basset knew we were here.

After breakfast we cleaned ourselves up and washed our shirts in a tub under the pump in the backyard. I borrowed a pair of scissors and cut Father's hair so it no longer hung limp and grey over his eyes. He looked more presentable and I no longer smelled of The Red Dragon. I would have liked to take Father for a bit of a walk but didn't want to run into the doctor so we sat on a bench in the landlady's backyard.

"I'm cold," Father said after a while, even though the sun was shining.

He went back to our room for a snooze and left me to my thoughts.

I hoped Mary was putting flowers on the graves as she'd promised. Although Mother had probably been removed from her grave long since, thanks to Jory and Dr. Basset. I didn't want to think about her being cut up by medical students and left who knows where. At least I knew where Henry was. What would he say if he could see me now? In my head, I heard his voice telling me that sometimes our imaginations made things seem worse than they really were. I hoped he was right.

* * *

"Shall we stay here?" Father asked, over breakfast the next morning.

I choked on my mouthful of bread and jam. Father thumped me on the back while I had a coughing fit. When I could breathe again, I wiped my eyes and sipped some water to give me time to think. Two days ago I would have jumped at the chance but why was Dr. Basset here?

"I'm sure we could find some kind of work," said Father. "And I don't want to get back on the ship."

"What about the mining company?"

"I know. It wouldn't be fair to them. It's funny though, I thought you'd jump at the chance to stay."

Could we stay without Dr. Basset finding us? If he'd asked our neighbours back home, they'd have told him we were sailing to Virgin Gorda so he had no reason to think we were in Quebec. But if he'd found out about the letter he might be angry and try to have Father locked away. Father was looking at me, waiting for me to say something. I fingered Mother's locket, remembering my promise.

"You'll be all right," I said. "Now that we've got you eating again." But would he? And what about me working at the mine! Should we go or should we stay? Father looked as unsure as I felt.

"I suppose I should honour that contract I signed," he said. "And I'm told it gets wickedly cold here in winter. At least the Virgin Islands will be warm."

I turned everything I knew over and over in my head as we packed up our belongings. What if it wasn't Dr. Basset I'd seen after all? Why was it so hard to make decisions? I never seemed to know what to do.

Thirty minutes later we walked up the Fortuna's gangplank. At the top I drew in a deep breath then slowly let it out. It was too late to change our minds now. Then it came to me in a flash that I'd been so taken aback at seeing Dr. Basset, I'd missed my chance to tell Father what happened to Henry. The only good thing was that we were about to leave the doctor behind.

Chapter 25

The sailors were stowing provisions and loading logs thicker than a man's body when we arrived back onboard ship. Pickersgill was wearing a thick jacket over a new woollen jersey and looked warm for the first time since we left Cornwall. I hoped that watching all the activity would keep Father's mind off seasickness. I grabbed his blanket, found him a sheltered place to sit and went to see if Mac had any hot water for tea. The captain found me in the galley.

"There you are Tremayne. What did you do with my sextant?"

"Your sextant, Sir?"

"You were taking readings with it as we approached Quebec. I can't find it anywhere."

"I left it in the wheelhouse, sir."

"You're sure?"

"Yes."

The captain gave me a searching look. "The helmsman said he hasn't seen it. In fact none of the crew have seen it since you were using it."

"But I wouldn't take it. What good would it be to me?"

"It was expensive. It wouldn't be hard to sell in a dockyard."

"I wouldn't do that, sir."

He studied my face for a few moments more.

"I hope not," he said, and left me alone in the galley.

My mouth was dry as I took Father a mug of sweet tea. What if the captain didn't believe me? What if he asked me to pay for a new sextant?

* * *

It took longer to load everything than expected and we spent another night at dock. At least this gave Father another calm night in the sheltered harbour. In the morning our pilot came aboard and there was a new flurry of activity as a tugboat attached a couple of lines. The tugboat puffed out black smoke and Father and I marvelled at the way it moved without sails or oars. The Fortuna was untied and the tug pulled us out into the wind. For better or worse, we were on our way and, despite all my problems, it was good to feel the ship swaying over the waves. My peace of mind lasted as long as it took me to glance back at the dock we had just left. Monsieur Renard, with his chewed ear, was shouting and pointing at the Fortuna. I turned to see what he was pointing at and had to clutch the side of the ship to keep my balance. I squeezed my eyes shut then opened them again to make sure they weren't playing tricks on me. Standing talking to the captain on the deck of the Fortuna was Dr. Basset. We should have jumped ship in Quebec after all.

When I felt as though my legs would support me, I moved over to a locker and sat down trying to think. There wasn't much point skipping roll call. If the doctor didn't already know Father and I were on board, he soon would. But why was he here?

I joined the inspection line and watched Dr. Basset's face, hoping to learn whether this was some weird coincidence. His face was thinner since our grave-robbing meeting and his eyes, with bruised bags beneath them, widened as they met mine.

"Mr. Tremayne!" he said.

He sounded genuinely surprised but could have been acting. It didn't take him long to recover his composure. When he peered inside my mouth he muttered, "I shall know if you tell anyone."

So he *didn't* know I'd already told someone?

Father greeted him as if he were an old friend and asked if he was going to Virgin Gorda, too.

"Not to stay," said Dr. Basset. "I thought I'd work aboard ship for a while, somewhere warm."

When we'd passed muster, I went in search of Hanna.

"Why is Dr. Basset on board?" I asked her.

"We always travel with a ship's doctor."

"What happened to the doctor who sailed to Quebec with us?"

"He's travelling on to Montreal."

"Why?"

"He has a position there. We knew he'd only be coming as far as Quebec."

"So when was Dr. Basset hired?"

"When we arrived."

"Isn't it unusual, changing doctors in the middle of a voyage?"

"Why all the questions?" asked Hanna. "Doctors work their passage all the time. We were lucky to find a replacement. It's not always easy."

Was it a coincidence that Dr. Basset was on our ship or had he signed on because he found out we were passengers?

"I heard that Mr. Hughes left without paying you," said Hanna. "I'm sorry."

"Not as sorry as I am." "Did you ever find out how his boar escaped from the pen?"

I shook my head. "Perhaps he let it out himself."

"Why would he do that?"

"For an excuse not to pay me."

"I suppose it's possible," said Hanna.

"Or perhaps it was Mr. Reddiman. He doesn't like me."

"He wouldn't put his crew in danger," said Hanna, frowning.

* * *

Despite his complaints about the cold, I kept Father out on deck as much as possible as we travelled down the St. Lawrence River. To my great relief, he took an interest in the passing shoreline and ships and chatted with the other miners. I took him to see the kittens in the galley where Mac showed us some small, green fruits.

"They're limes," he said. "From a ship just back from Jamaica. They'll put an end to your scurvy."

On alternate mornings, for as long as they lasted, he gave Father one to squeeze into a mug of water. Father made a face when he sipped the first one and stirred in several spoonfuls of sugar before he drank it but his teeth no longer wobbled and bled when he ate. After the limes were all gone, I gave him the dried berries and he chewed on a few of those each morning.

Five days after we left, a schooner picked up our pilot and the next day we headed into open sea. The wind gained strength and blew the waves higher. There was lots of chop and every roll of the ship sent sea water sloshing across her deck. I watched Father anxiously but his sea sickness didn't return. He ate small but proper meals and his skin lost its grey colour. He spent most of his days in the dining room and saloon talking to the other miners and playing card games and dominoes. I caught up on my diary entries and Emile helped me hem Hanna's birthday present.

"Are you afraid of anything?" I asked, as Emile undid a knot in my thread.

He thought about this.

"I'm afraid of spendin' all my days in the same place doin' the same things."

"But is there anything that makes your head spin and your legs give way?"

"I 'spect there is. Everyone's afraid of somethin'. But I ain't come across it yet."

"Is it better to face something you're afraid of or avoid it?"

Emile thought for a moment as he handed Hanna's shawl back to me.

"No point scarin' yourself silly. I knowed people scared so bad they lost their minds. Now don't pull the thread so tight."

At night I wrestled with questions I couldn't answer. What was Dr. Basset doing in The Red Dragon and why was Monsieur Renard so angry about the doctor leaving aboard the Fortuna? Had the doctor joined our ship to keep me quiet or was he on the run? It would be hard to catch up to a man who kept changing ship and he certainly kept to himself. I hadn't seen him since roll call when we left Quebec.

There were so many things I didn't know. Things like what I was going to do when we reached Virgin Gorda and how I was going to tell Father it was my fault Henry went back into the mine alone and drowned.

Chapter 26

It seemed there was nothing I could do about Dr. Basset, and I didn't have to worry about Father dying now that he was over his seasickness and gaining weight, so I grappled with the problem of Virgin Gorda. I enjoyed helping out around the ship but could hardly ask for payment, especially when the sailors were taking time to show me how to raise and lower sails, splice sheets, and do all the other tasks that filled their days and nights. If I couldn't pay off my passage, I'd have to work for the mining company but what if the mine captain wouldn't give me a job above ground? Perhaps the owners would let me pay them back a bit at a time if I could find some other work on the island. Then again, apart from mining and pigs, the only thing I knew anything about was sailing. Hanna's words, "you could be captain of this ship," came back to me. Perhaps I could make a life for myself at sea.

The need to do something about my problems and the lack of any better alternatives gave me the courage to report to the captain one sunny morning when we were scudding along at a spanking pace. He was in his cabin and answered my knock saying "Come." His face tightened when he saw me but I spoke before he could say anything.

"Sir, I'll swear on the Bible I didn't steal your sextant and I'll be very careful to return anything I use to you personally if only you'll continue to teach me."

The captain launched into a lecture about the cost and importance of reliable instruments and charts, and dire circumstances that could arise should those items be lost at sea while we were unable to replace them. I sat wide-eyed and nodded now and again to show I was paying attention. When he'd finished, he began to explain the chart he'd been studying that was unrolled across his desk. He didn't mention the missing sextant again. I waited a few days until his eagerness to share his seemingly endless knowledge with me had returned before asking what was on my mind.

"Sir, could someone like me become captain of a ship?"

I had just written our latest position in the ship's log and he watched me carefully blot my entry before answering.

"I don't see why not. You can read and write. You pick things up quickly enough."

"How would I start?"

"At the bottom."

"How would I get a job at the bottom?"

"Unless you have a relative in the business, you'd have to find someone in need of a ship's boy. You wouldn't want to sign on with just anyone though. Some captains are notoriously cruel and won't hesitate to put a sailor's life in danger." He tapped one foot while he thought. "Is this something you particularly want to do?"

"I hate mining, sir."

"Only it's not an easy life. And it takes time to rise through the ranks."

"I feel as though I belong at sea."

"Then sail back with me. I won't be able to pay you without a vacant position for you to fill, but I'll feed you and help you sign on with another ship once we reach England."

I longed to say yes. Just once it would be good to do what *I* wanted without having to consider anyone or anything else.

"I wish I could but I'll owe the mining company for my passage. I doubt they'll let me sail away without paying them."

And if I went anyway Father would have to face their wrath.

"Then I'll be back to the Virgin Islands next year. If you still want to sign on, I could take you back with me then."

Surely a year would be enough to pay off what I owed. Then I'd be free of mines forever. And if Father was settled?

"Oh yes. Thank you sir."

Perhaps my optimism was helped by rising temperatures and sunny skies but I began to feel that things might work out.

* * *

Early one morning, when I'd finished peeling a mound of potatoes, I lifted one of Tiger's kittens onto my lap. Although Tiger wouldn't allow us to pet him, or rather her, she didn't seem to mind us handling her kittens.

"I can't decide whether their eyes are going to be green or gold," I said, as I wiped away beads of sweat about to trickle into my eyes. "They must be very hot with all their fur."

"Aye," said Mac. "It gets hot as Hades in here but if Tiger thinks it's too hot for his family, he'll move out." Mac glanced at my woollen trousers and work shirt.

"You could take your shirt off, laddie."

It was all right for Mac. *His* chest was broad and muscular.

"I don't like to," I said.

"Oh?"

"I get teased a lot."

"Hauling on the lines will help fill you out." Mac waggled a piece of cord and the kitten pounced on it.

"It's not that. It's ... well, I have this birthmark shaped like an earwig."

And that's what the bullies back home called me, Irwyn the earwig. They said it would crawl into my ear one day and gnaw through my brain.

"And where is this birthmark?"

"Just below my rib here." I pulled up my shirt to show Mac.

"It does look like an earwig," said Mac, peering closely, "but I could change it into something else."

"Change what?" asked Hanna, coming into the galley.

My face grew even hotter as I quickly tucked my shirt back into my trousers.   "Change it how?" I asked.

"Mac gestured towards the mermaid lounging along his left bicep.

"Did you do that?"

"No, but a Chinese sailor taught me how."

"He's tattooed some of Fortuna's crew," said Hanna, cuddling the ginger kitten with white paws. "I want to have a butterfly but the captain won't let me."

"What could you make of my earwig?"

"A sea serpent," said Mac.

"I'm not very fond of snakes."

"You could have an eagle," said Hanna. "Or you like pigs."

I could just imagine the names I'd be called if I had a pig tattooed on my stomach. I shook my head.

"How about a scorpion," said Mac.

"What's a scorpion?"

"A creature about the size of my hand with claws and a tail held high." Mac held up his fist with curved outside fingers extended. "It carries a nasty sting in its tail so other creatures will nae mess with it."

Perhaps a scorpion would help me to be more decisive and take charge of my life.

* * *

Mac tattooed me that evening after supper. He'd wanted to do it on deck during daylight hours but I didn't want people watching and I didn't want Father trying to stop me either. Hanna took us to a musty-smelling unoccupied cabin. We moved some crates aside so I could lie on the bunk while Mac got to work with his needle. I suppose I should have realized that having a needle stuck into my belly over and over again was going to hurt.

"Have you almost finished?" I asked, trying to blink away tears before they rolled down my face.

"Nae, we've a way to go yet," Mac said.

"He's done half the outline," said Hanna. Her expression, lit up by the lantern she was holding, showed a mixture of fascination and envy. "It's really good. You'll love it."

I was relieved to hear this. Especially with Mac muttering "uh oh" or "steady now" each time the Fortuna rolled over a particularly large wave. I tried to distract myself by counting the number of knotholes in the cabin walls.

What seemed like hours later, Mac put his needle down and said he was finished.

I sat up and looked at the oozing black mess. What had I done?

"Don't worry laddie," Mac said, taking a look at my face. "It'll look fine when it's healed. Wash it three times a day with soap and water until it heals. The salt water will sting but keep it from festering."

I wished Mac and Hanna goodnight and made my way along the passageway. As I stumbled a second time, I placed a hand on the wall for balance. Was the ship pitching more than usual or was I a bit dizzy? I continued on towards raised voices coming through an open doorway.

"You're wrong," said one. "Or is this Tremayne's work?"

I paused at mention of my name.

"They are *my* calculations and they are correct," said the captain.

"They can't be."

"I am captain of this ship and it is not your place to question my orders."

A red-faced Mr. Reddiman stormed into the passageway, glared at me, then stomped off. When I reached our bunk, I was glad to find Father already asleep. At least he wouldn't want to know where I'd been all evening. My tattoo burned like a sunburn but I fell asleep anyway. I woke to the sensation of being in mid air.

Chapter 27

I plunged back towards my bunk and landed with a thunk that threatened to rearrange my bones. Wind wailed through the rigging. Someone was sobbing and Father moaned.

"How long have we been pitching like this?" I grabbed the sides of my bunk as my body threatened to become airborne again.

"Ages," said Father, although I think I'd have woken sooner if that were true. "I'm sorry son." The Fortuna plunged down and down, her timbers creaking.

Sorry for what? Were we sinking?

"I'll find out what's happening," I said, wishing Hanna had got around to that swimming lesson she'd promised.

I clambered upright with some difficulty and remembered my tattoo as I slammed into a post. In a moment's lull as the ship sat in the bottom of a trough, I heard voices muttering the Lord's Prayer. Then the Fortuna gathered herself with a groan and shuddered up the next wave.

I felt my way around, grabbing hold of whatever I could with one hand before I let go with the other. I didn't want to rearrange my scorpion on some immovable object or bash my brains out. Although that might be preferable to drowning. At least I wouldn't know what was happening.

"Oi!"

I jumped. In the dark, I'd accidently grabbed someone's shoulder.

"Sorry," I said.

"Careful lad." He held onto my wrist until I'd found something else to grab onto.

The conversation I'd heard between the captain and Mr. Reddiman before I'd gone to bed flashed into my head. Were we off course? Somewhere we shouldn't be?

It worked best if I moved when the Fortuna was climbing up or plunging down a wave. When she pitched over the top or thudded into a trough, I simply hung on to whatever I could. It was slow going and exhausting. Thumps and shouts came from above and I realized the deck might not be the best place for me. Instead, I made my way to the galley and was relieved to find Mac there. He was securing cupboards and drawers so they wouldn't spill their contents if the catches gave way.

"It's all right laddie," he said, when he caught sight of me in the doorway. "A wee bit of a storm, that's all." He looked reassuringly unflustered by the ship's violent pitching. "Give me a hand."

I picked my way amongst pots and knives that were sliding across the galley floor.

"We're not sinking then?"

"Och, the Fortuna can handle a lot worse than this. Here, tie this canister in place."

He gave me a length of cord and I silently thanked Emile for teaching me some mariners' knots.

"How long will it last?"

"It's hard to say. We don't often see storms here at this time of year. But if it's breakfast you're wanting you'll have to make do with a biscuit or two."

He nodded towards a large metal pot, tied to a post, that was full of ship's biscuits.

"I can help if you want to cook porridge."

"Och, we'd set the ship ablaze if we lit the stove in this. You can take the biscuits to the dining room in case anyone else is up and about."

I untied the pot.

"Oh, and don't think of going out on deck," Mac called after me. "The crew have enough to do without passengers thrashing about and falling overboard."

I clutched the pot against my stomach. Holding onto the ship was tricky with only one free hand and I'd gained more bruises by the time I reached the dining room. Someone had tied the water barrel to a table leg. I tied the pot to another table leg, half-filled a mug with water, sat on the floor, and unbuttoned my shirt. My tattoo still looked a mess but I couldn't fetch salt water to wash it without going on deck and God forbid Mac should find me using our precious fresh water. I bit into a biscuit and almost broke my front teeth. I struck the biscuit against the floor. A weevil fell out but the biscuit didn't break. I put it in my mug and, after a minute or two, it was oatmeal mush that tasted nowhere near as good as Mac's porridge but stopped my stomach from rumbling. I ate two more biscuits in this way, then softened up another to take back to Father.

"We're about to drown and you're worried about eating," he said, as he pushed away the mug of mush I offered.

"We're not about to drown. Mac said so."

Father gripped the sides of his bunk as the Fortuna slammed into waves that rolled her both sideways and bow to stern.

I would have liked to go up on deck but mindful of Mac's orders I made my way back to the saloon where I wedged myself between the wall and a post and hoped Father wouldn't start vomiting his guts up again. A few miners had gathered in the adjoining dining room. I sat where I was on the floor until the captain came to ask those of us feeling well enough to take a turn at the pumps.

We stood knee deep in water in the hold and the sailor in charge sang slow songs to keep us pumping in rhythm. I joined in when I'd learned the choruses and took shifts until

I couldn't lift my arms any more. Before I left, I pulled up my shirt and sloshed a handful of scummy seawater over my tattoo. Back in steerage, the effort of undressing was too much. I tied myself into my bunk with my blanket and slept.

A terrific crash woke me up.

Chapter 28

The entire ship shuddered with the crash. I leapt out of bed but found myself dangling over the side of my bunk with my feet caught in my blanket. Oh, right. Last night I'd tied myself in. I think someone screamed but it was hard to hear over the shriek of the wind and the Fortuna's groans and thumps. I untangled myself and rushed up to the deck. At least I tried to rush. The ship plunged and rolled more than ever. Twice I stumbled to my knees and slid across the floor, my arms held out so I wouldn't bang into anything. I reached the door that led onto the main deck, grabbed the door handle then hesitated. If we were sinking, I should have brought Father with me. But surely there'd be time to go back and fetch him. Wouldn't there?

I turned the handle and tried to push the door open. It was stuck. Were we locked in, or had something fallen against the door? I leaned all my weight against it and it gave, suddenly, so I stumbled over the lip of the doorway. The wind wrenched the door out of my hand, slammed it open then smashed it against my shoulder. The deck tilted and a two-foot wave rolled towards me. I grabbed the door and slammed it shut as Mac's instructions about not going out on deck lit up in my head. The wave broke against me and the door. I wiped my dripping face and felt something dangle over my head. Rigging. The mainmast had snapped. Sailors were shouting at each other as they cut away tangled shrouds to salvage what they could of the sails but it was impossible to hear what they said over the roaring, splattering, and banging. Wind whipped the canvas and it was all they could do to stop it from blowing overboard.

Intending to help untangle the debris, I gripped the handrail with both hands. The wind practically blew me up the stairs to the poop deck. I reached the top as we plunged down another wave. My right foot caught in a rope coil and my backside hit the deck. I struggled to free my foot and the Fortuna tilted again as she climbed the next wave. I began to slide backwards. My foot, still caught, pulled a mess of rope and splintered wood behind me as I slid on my back, head first, towards the stern.

I slid alongside the wheelhouse struggling to sit up so I wouldn't smash my head, then stopped short. A splintered spar had caught across the base of the mizzenmast. The deck levelled momentarily as we crested the wave. I struggled to my feet and hung on, waterlogged and shaking. How was I going to make my way forward again?

The wind subsided for a moment and a new noise caught my attention. The helmsman was banging on the wheelhouse window. He shouted something I couldn't hear and beckoned. It took all my courage to let go of the ship's side and lunge for the wheelhouse door. Then I was out of the wind and spray and the helmsman was shouting.

"Go and get help."

His face was haggard.

"I sent Pickersgill to find another helmsman ages ago. I've been on the wheel for hours. I'm exhausted."

It was warm in the wheelhouse. My battered body sagged towards the floor. The helmsman wiped a layer of sweat from his forehead with a shaking hand.

"If I don't keep her heading into the waves we'll swamp."

That straightened me up again. Someone had to get help and there was only me. I wondered what had happened to Pickersgill as I stepped out into the maelstrom and waited for the right moment to let go of the door. There was a lull in the wind and I lunged towards the side of the ship and began to drag myself forward. I made slow progress battling against the wind but didn't want to risk being knocked off my feet again. I willed the helmsman to hang on. Then Emile was up ahead stuffing sails into a locker. I clamped a hand on his shoulder to get his attention.

"We need another helmsman," I shouted

"Find Mr. Reddiman," Emile shouted back. "Try the saloon."

I battled my way back below deck. My face stung from the wind and it was a relief to be inside again. Mr. Reddiman *was* in the saloon kneeling beside a sailor who lay on the floor.

"The helmsman's all in," I said, my voice sounding loud without the competing wind. "He can't hang on much longer."

Mr. Reddiman uttered an oath I didn't catch as he scrambled to his feet. He grabbed my arm, pulled me to the door, then whispered, "Stay with able seaman Jones. He was caught under the mainmast when it broke and he's in a bad way. Dr. Basset's been sent for."

Then he rushed off.

I knelt in Mr. Reddiman's place. The right side of the sailor's chest looked oddly flat. His shoulder was soaked in blood and his right arm lay at an unnatural angle. Pink, foamy spittle dribbled from one corner of his mouth.

"The doctor's on his way," I said, hoping this was true.

The sailor's eye's flickered open and with a move so sudden it made me jump, he grabbed at my sleeve with his good hand. We were staring at each other when Dr. Basset arrived. He ran a hand over the sailor's smashed shoulder and rib cage. The sailor groaned. The doctor took a flask from his pocket and lifted the sailor's head so he could drink but it mostly ran down his chin. From the smell, I guessed it was rum. The doctor looked at me and shook his head.

"Help me get him to bed."

We should have left him where he was. His screams, as we lifted him, made me shiver. But we managed to tuck him up in a cabin next to the doctor's. We placed folded blankets between his smashed shoulder and the edge of the bunk. The doctor soaked a clean handkerchief in rum, gave it to the sailor to suck on, and handed me the flask.

"Give him as much as he wants," he said, then left.

The sailor's breathing was so shallow it was hard to detect any movement. If only there was something I could do. I took his good hand in mine and began to recite the Lord's Prayer.

Chapter 29

I don't know how long I knelt beside the injured sailor's bunk with an extra blanket hung across my sodden shoulders before I nodded off. The creak of the cabin door opening woke me and I instantly realized two things. The first was that the thumping and crashing of past days had been replaced by subdued scrapings and voices that weren't shouting. The storm was over.

The second thing I realized was that the injured sailor was dead.

"Just as well," said Dr. Basset. "I couldn't have saved his shoulder and his crushed ribs must have punctured one of his lungs."

I uncurled the sailor's stiffening fingers from my hand as pins and needles stabbed my feet. When I could stand, I went to check on Father.

He was asleep with our water jug wedged between him and the corner of his bunk. Being careful not to wake him, I took it up on deck to empty out his vomit. Everything was white with crusted salt including the tangled web of rigging. The deck was strewn with wreckage shivered into bits. There was only three feet or so of the main mast left and the mizzenmast was cracked. Emile was sorting through a heap of shredded sails.

"Seaman Jones is dead," I told him. Emile nodded.

"Do you know where he lived?"

Emile shook his head. "He wasn't much of a talker."

"Anyone else hurt?"

"A crushed finger, a broken ankle. Nothin' serious."

"What about Pickersgill?"

"Huh."

"What d'you mean, huh?"

"He was hidin'. Too scared to come on deck. He says he hit his head and was knocked out but no one believes him."

I picked up a sail from the salvageable pile and threaded one of Emile's stout needles. Trying not to break the blisters I'd rubbed whilst manning the pumps, I began to sew up a tear.

"Here." Emile passed me a thick leather glove so I could push the needle through the stiff canvas without taking more skin off my hands. The carpenters were already at work fashioning new masts.

"It's lucky we took all that wood on board in Quebec," I said.

"A good captain always has the makins of spare parts stowed on his ship," said Emile.

The usually cheery sailors wore glum faces. At first I thought this was due to exhaustion and the amount of work needed to make the Fortuna shipshape again. Then I saw the great mats of weed floating in troughs between the waves.

"Where are we?" I asked.

"The Sargasso Sea."

But I'd heard about strange mats of weed floating on the sea somewhere and my brain suddenly made the connection.

"In the Devil's Triangle?"

Emile nodded.

"Where there's no wind, and ships and their men simply disappear?"

"Well we ain't disappeared yet," said Emile.

"And we still have wind."

But Emile shook his head. "No we don't. We just sloppin' up and down on the waves."

I licked my finger and held it up. Emile was right. There was no wind.

"So why have we got waves if there's no wind."

"It takes a while for the sea to settle after a storm like that."

"Are you worried?"

"Ain't much point worryin'. It won't change nothin.'"

Emile began to mend another sail. I tried to copy his neat stitches.

"How you and your daddy goin' to live when you get to Virgin Gorda?"

"I don't know."

"Only my brother, Rémy, he has extra rooms. He's a good cook and he like to have company. If you and your daddy want to live with Rémy it would help him out."

"What does Rémy do?"

"He used to work on a sugar plantation but it closed down. Now he pick up a job here and there and he nurse people when they sick.

"What work is there on the island besides the mine?"

"Not much. We used to grow sugar and cotton but since the slaves were freed four years ago the plantation owners, they can't make money no more. Then there's the rain."

"What about the rain?"

"Bad storms that flatten the crops. Or no rain at all."

The news was going from bad to worse. Not only were we stuck in the Devil's Triangle but it was unlikely I'd find work outside the mine.

"I'll ask Father where we're going to live."

"Then tell your daddy our house look way out over the ocean and Rémy, he make the best conch chowder anyone ever tasted."

* * *

Later, Hanna came to find me.

It's time for that swimming lesson I promised you," she said.

There was a sizeable gap in the weed mats along one side of the ship. I looked at the possibly bottomless water then gestured towards the yards of torn canvas lying on the deck.

"We have all these to mend."

"Don't worry," said Emile. "We'll get through them."

I'd already burst a couple of blisters, despite the borrowed glove. And it would be comforting to know I could swim if we sailed through another storm.

"Take care of this for me," I said, as I hung Mother's locket round Emile's neck. It was the first time I'd taken it off since leaving home and I didn't want to lose it. I peeled off my shirt and followed Hanna to an open gate in the bulwark. She handed me a plank of wood.

"Now hold onto this plank and jump in," she said. "Hold your breath as you go under and you'll quickly pop up again"

I looked at her." Aren't you coming in?"

"Of course. I'll go first if you like. Hold your nose so the water doesn't shoot up it."

"What about sharks?"

My question was too late. She'd already jumped over the side. She bobbed up moments later.

"Come on," she shouted.

I tried to swallow but my mouth was too dry. My feet wouldn't move.

Hanna waved and grinned. Two hands shoved me in the back and I was falling. I clutched the plank with both hands and water shot up my nose. I bobbed to the surface, coughing, and Hanna grabbed hold of me.

"Who .... was that?" I gasped.

"Pickersgill," said Hanna. "He must have thought you needed help getting in. Now hold the plank beneath your chest. That's it. And kick your legs. Like this."

After a few minutes of splashing and spluttering I figured out how to keep my head above water. Then Hanna took the plank away.

"You don't need it," she said. "Paddle your arms, like this,"

But waves kept slopping into my face and my arms were still sore from pumping. After a few minutes of thrashing about she towed me to a rope ladder and said that was enough for one day.

* * *

Changed into dry clothes, I sat with Father in the dining room. He'd finished the last of the berries and I didn't want the scurvy coming back so I was relieved to see that he'd recovered enough from the storm to eat a small helping of Mac's octopus stew. We were still sitting over our bowls when the captain asked for everyone's attention.

"We've plenty of provisions and water so don't worry about the lack of wind. We can make good use of this calm spell to repair the damage from the storm, however my tired crew would welcome any help you can give them. There is also a less pleasant matter that I need your help with. I regret to tell you that we have a thief on board. A sextant was stolen from the ship when we reached Quebec and, since then, several crew members have had personal belongings disappear."

The murmur of whispered conversations began and the captain held up his hand for silence.

"I shall find out who this thief is and the sooner I find out the better. So if you see anything suspicious, or have any knowledge that may be pertinent to this matter, you must come and tell me. There will be serious consequences for anyone who tries to shield the person responsible for this thievery. Thank you."

Chapter 30

By morning the sea had flattened out and we were still becalmed. Emile set me to work beside Hanna, cutting frayed ropes and splicing the sound pieces together again. He took Father over to help the carpenters. The Fortuna was in a patch of clear water but six men rowed one of the ship's boats to some nearby weed mats dragging a net.

"So that's how they caught the octopus for yesterday's stew," I said. "We could do with some fishing lines."

"You wouldn't catch anything," said Hanna. "There are octopus and shrimps and crabs but, strangely, no fish."

When we'd finished, Hanna offered to give me another swimming lesson. I hung Mother's locket around Father's neck then took off my shirt and tied the arms around a post. This was more from habit than necessity. There was not the lightest flicker of a breeze, but I had learned that anything left on the deck of a ship was best fastened down.

Not wanting to give Pickersgill the pleasure of pushing me again, I jumped in quickly and held my nose so I wasn't coughing water out of my lungs when I surfaced. We paddled for a while with me holding the plank beneath my chest. It was easier to breathe without waves slopping into my face. Next Hanna got me to turn over onto my back.

"Lie back in the water," she said, as I strained to hold my head up. "You won't sink."

To my surprise, I didn't. We floated alongside a weed bed where tiny crabs and eels were at home.

"Do you think it's better to face something scary and unpleasant, or avoid it"

"Depends what it is," said Hanna. "I'd rather avoid snakes, even harmless ones. They give me the shivers."

Knowing that I could float on my back gave me the courage to try swimming on my front again. It wasn't pretty, but I managed a lap around the Fortuna. When I tried to climb the rope ladder, however, my triumph turned to embarrassment. My arms and legs shook so much that Hanna had to haul me back on board. I lay on my back trying to summon up the energy to move. Hanna's wet clothes clung to the swell of her breasts and the curve of hips that were normally hidden by her loose clothing. Aware that my wet trousers must be clinging in an equally revealing way, I rolled onto my stomach.

"I'll lie here in the sun for a while and dry off," I said.

Hanna muttered something about getting changed and padded away. When my back had dried I went to sit beside

Father. He was taking a break from carpentry by way of a snooze in the sun. He woke as I sat down and nodded towards my tattoo. "What on earth's that?" he asked.

"A scorpion. Mac did it."

It had almost healed and looked much better than it had before the storm. Even so, Father gave me a searching look. Before he could say anything more, I began to tell him about Emile's brother, Rémy.

"Well," said Father, "that would solve one problem on my mind."

He cleared his throat. He'd quickly got over his bout of seasickness during the storm. Even so, his ribs stood out like an old nag's bound for the knacker's yard and I hoped Emile was right about his brother's cooking. Father cleared his throat again.

"Shall I fetch a mug of tea?" I asked.

"No, I, um, I've something to say to you."

"Oh?"

"You've finally started to grow."

"I have?"

Father unrolled one of my trouser legs. Instead of reaching my ankle, as it had when we left home, it was part way up my calf.

"Hanna's a bright young girl. I can see she likes you."

I had a horrible feeling I knew where this conversation was going.

"But she's only thirteen and she's grown up without a mother. You must keep this in mind and act, well … responsibly."

I almost laughed. "There's little chance to be anything else. It's impossible to be alone on this ship." As the words left my lips, I realized this probably wasn't the reassurance Father was looking for. I also realized that the two miners' wives standing at the rail nearby had stopped their lively conversation and had their heads turned a little towards us. "And there's always someone listening," I said, a little louder. I jumped to my feet. "I need to put my shirt on. I'm getting sunburned."

I was already at my bunk when I realized my shirt was still up on deck. As I turned to retrace my steps, another picture of Father's bony chest popped into my head and I realized something was wrong. I went charging back up to the deck.

"Where's my locket," I yelled.

Father put down the piece of wood he'd just resumed shaping while one hand groped around his neck but nothing was there. He looked down at his bare chest and back at me.

"The chain must have broken," he said, frowning.

We searched the deck and asked everyone if they'd seen the locket but no one had.

"It must be here somewhere," Father said. "It's a good job it's calm. Someone will find it."

But the chain was well made. I was sure it hadn't broken. Someone must have taken it while Father slept.

* * *

Mr. Reddiman was using Pickersgill to fetch and carry. When men went aloft to mend the rigging, Pickersgill had to climb up to where they were working. He went up and down, up and down, until I almost felt sorry for him. I'm sure the sailors were asking for tools they didn't need, or had forgotten on purpose, for the pleasure of making him climb up and down one more time.

"I suppose that's his punishment for hiding during the storm," I said to Emile, one sweaty afternoon, as Pickersgill struggled aloft yet again.

"He's either lazy or scared," said Emile. "Either way, we don't want our lives to be in the hands of someone who don't do his job properly. Mr. Reddiman goin' to make or break him."

Mr. Reddiman had been in a foul mood since the storm. I'd heard the sailors muttering together when they thought no one else was around. Coupled with what I'd heard the night I was tattooed, I gathered Mr. Reddiman blamed the captain for steering us off course and into the storm. Still, with everyone helping, the repairs progressed quickly and by evening the Fortuna was more or less shipshape again.

The following day, while I was eating breakfast, I heard a commotion on deck. I rushed out to see ripples on the water and the sailors were raising sails. As soon as we were underway we had a short ceremony and Seaman Jones, neatly sewn into sailcloth along with a couple of stones, was lowered overboard.

Chapter 31

July eleventh was Hanna's fourteenth birthday but it began with chores like any other day. Mr. Reddiman wanted to check that a repair in the hull above the waterline was holding. As usual, when there was an unpleasant job to be done, he called for Pickersgill, who was helped into the bosun's chair. This seat was a plank of wood. Woven ropes formed the sides, front and back. Long ropes extended from either side so the chair could be hoisted into the rigging or lowered over the side. Even though the winds were light, the chair swung like a pendulum and Pickersgill clutched the ropes with white knuckles.

"Don't worry," shouted one of the sailors lowering the chair, "We only let go when it's someone we don't like."

Pickersgill looked up, amidst unkind laughter, and his eyes met mine. It's a good job looks can't really kill. Taken aback by his poisonous expression, I turned away from the rail. Was he mad at me? I didn't like him but couldn't think of any reason I'd given him to hate me. I was distracted from my thoughts by the sight of a ship off our stern that had drawn closer overnight. Her lines were sleek and a mass of sails gave her more speed than we could muster. It would be fun to sail on her.

Later, I decorated the dining room with the Fortuna's flags while Mac cooked pork with beans and rice for supper. Afterwards there was a pudding with glacé cherries and the sweet treacle-like syrup I'd tasted in Quebec. I asked Mac what it was.

"Maple tree sap," he said.

After supper, passengers and crew members alike brought their musical instruments out on deck and began to play. The wind had died during the afternoon and the deck was cleared for dancing. Just about everyone was there except Dr. Basset. I don't know what he found to do all day and night in his cabin.

Father clapped and sang and tapped his toes in time to the music. Hanna had the first dance with the captain but there was no spring to his step and he went to find a seat as soon as the tune ended. I was about to take his place when Pickersgill rushed up and took Hanna's hand. Not wanting to watch him with Hanna I moved away and caught sight of Emile.

"Did Hanna like her birthday present?" asked Emile.

"I haven't given it to her," I said.

"But you work so hard on it," said Emile.

"I know. It seemed like a good idea when we were in Quebec but now that the days are hot and sunny and the nights are warm too, she doesn't need a warm shawl or an extra blanket."

"It don't matter. It goin' to get cold again when she sails back to England. Besides, it's the thought that counts."

Emile was right. And I wasn't going to get what I wanted out of life by standing around watching. When the musicians stopped for refreshments I took Hanna aside and gave her the shawl.

"Thank you Irwyn," she said. "Did you sew this yourself?"

"Emile helped me."

She must have noticed that the stitches had been unpicked and re-sewn several times in my efforts to keep them all the same size, but all she said was, "This is very thoughtful of you."

Then she gave me a quick hug and I wished there weren't so many people around because I would have liked to kiss her. I did dance with her though, when the musicians resumed. Pickersgill had disappeared. I learned later that he'd been sent to the galley to wash the supper dishes.

A mist rolled in as the hour grew late. The musicians packed away their instruments and people drifted off to bed. Hearing Father sing had brought back memories of him being in the church choir. When had he given that up? I sifted through memories like the wisps of mist that trailed through the rigging.

I didn't hear Hanna's approach and jumped when she spoke.

"I have this odd feeling," she said, "that nothing will ever be the same after this voyage."

Were those tears in her eyes? With no wind, the only sailors left on deck were the night watch and, as I couldn't see them, I assumed they couldn't see us. I took a step towards Hanna and stumbled over something. It was the bosun's chair.

"Pickersgill should have put it away," I said.

"Why does everyone blame Pickersgill for everything?" asked Hanna.

"Because he doesn't pull his weight."

"But everyone picks on him. He used to work in a bakery and was happy there but the baker died and his uncle made him take this job. He hates it."

I knew what that was like. I could still picture his white knuckles gripping the ropes on the bosun's chair and the look on his pale face.

"I suppose it was a bit scary," I said.

"What was scary?, asked Hanna.

"Swinging around inches above the sea, banging into the hull, and praying he wouldn't fall in."

"That's not scary."

"If he can't swim it would be." "There's no way a person can fall out of that chair."

Obviously I did not look convinced.

"Okay," said Hanna, climbing into the chair.

"What are you doing?"

"Showing you this isn't scary. Now lower me over the side."

"No way."

"Afraid you're not strong enough?"

I should have known better but, spurred on by the holiday mood of the evening and having drunk toasts to Hanna's health, our wonderful captain, his fine crew, Mac's excellent supper and the talented musicians, and having finally had chance to hold Hanna in my arms while we danced, common sense had deserted me. I wound the chair's ropes around a belaying pin and looked down into the mist.

"How will I know when to stop lowering you?"

"I'll tug on the rope," said Hanna, balancing on the side of the ship. "One tug to stop lowering, two to haul me back up. Ready?"

I gripped the ropes and braced myself as she disappeared over the side. I couldn't see her from where I stood so I lowered slowly and tried to gauge how much rope I'd let out. I was just thinking that she'd proved her point and I should haul her back up anyway when I felt a tug, heard a muffled "oh", and the ropes went loose. I pulled them up. They'd been cut. Right above the chair. As I stared at them, trying to take in what had happened, a cry went up from the watch.

"Ship to starboard."

Through a gap in the mist I glimpsed a ship's rigging alongside ours. And Dr. Basset. How long had he been on deck? He was staring across a few feet of water to my old "friend" with the chewed-up ear. Then he turned towards me. I looked back at the other ship, trying desperately to understand what was happening. Something smashed into my skull.

Chapter 32

Everything was black when I opened my eyes. I tried to lift my hands to my face but couldn't. They were tied. My ankles were tied, too. How long had I been tied up? And where was I? On a bunk, but not my bunk. It didn't smell right. I knew that smell though. What was it? Then it came to me. The smoky smell from The Red Dragon. Which was odd because I couldn't be in The Red Dragon. But Hanna. She'd disappeared. I had to tell the Captain.

I lifted my head then lowered it as pain throbbed above my ear. I tried to think. I rolled towards my left side and felt the lump of my knife sheath. Was my knife still inside? I rolled onto my back again, lifted my hips and began to jiggle them. The knife moved. I strained to lift my hips higher and jiggled some more. On the third try, my knife slid out of its sheath and landed on the mattress with a soft plop. I shuffled my backside up towards my right hand and brought my head down towards my knees. I couldn't quite reach it. I shuffled a bit more. Ropes bit into my wrists and ankles as I strained to reach. I closed my lips over the hilt. I had it. I brought my face over to my left hand then stopped. Which side was the sharpened edge of the blade? If only I could see!

I tried to picture the knife hilt and felt its curve with my tongue. The sharp edge was on the left. Or was it? If I had it the wrong way round I would slice my wrist open. I pulled on the rope that secured my left hand and carefully inserted the knife blade between the rope and my wrist. I clamped my teeth around the hilt and slowly drew the knife up along the rope. The blade was cold and blunt against my skin. I let out the breath I'd been holding and began to saw at the rope. I tried not to think about how quickly I would bleed to death if the knife slipped.

Something gave but the rope still held. My right arm was about to pull out of its socket. I sawed faster. The rope gave a bit more. My teeth ached and my lips were going numb. I bit harder on the hilt. How thick was this rope? I sawed up, down, up, down. The hilt slipped. It jabbed against the roof of my mouth. My head jerked back. The knife slid from my numb lips. No! I yanked on the rope in frustration. The last strand gave way. My left hand was free. I wriggled my fingers to bring feeling back into them. Then I picked up my knife and sliced my other hand free, then my feet. I stood up and, trying not to make any noise, groped for the door.

The hallway lantern shone into Dr. Basset's cabin. Why would Dr. Basset knock me out and tie me up? And what did The Red Dragon's Monsieur Renard have to do with Dr. Basset and his body snatching? Now Hanna had been snatched. But she wasn't dead, was she? I had to find the captain but what was I going to tell him when I found him?

The door to the captain's cabin was ajar and someone - Dr. Basset - was talking.

"They're lying. They're just saying their captain is injured to get me aboard."

"And why would they want you aboard," asked the captain, "if they don't need a doctor?"

"How the hell would I know what devious scheme they've hatched. They're smugglers."

"How do *you* know?"

"Just look at them. Besides, honest men don't take young girls hostage."

"Which is why I have to get Hanna back before they harm her," said the captain. "They're demanding your help in exchange for her and I have no other choice but to agree. You must see that."

My brain was working overtime. Hanna was on the other ship. It must have been Renard's men who cut the bosun's chair loose. Because … they want the doctor? And … he doesn't want to tell the captain why … but he's afraid of them. I heard someone behind me. I whirled around, an action that set my head throbbing again.

"What are you doing?" asked Mr. Reddiman, glaring at me.

The captain appeared in the doorway. Dr. Basset was right behind him. I wanted to tell the captain not to trust the doctor, but could he still have Father put away?

"Then I shall need an assistant," said Dr. Basset. "I'll take Irwyn with me."

What could I say? Would the captain believe me if I told him the doctor was a body snatcher who smoked opium.

"Irwyn, the men on the other ship are rough scoundrels," said the captain. "You don't have to go with the doctor if you don't want to."

But I did have to go. Henry had died because I acted like a coward. I couldn't make that mistake again. Especially when it was my fault that Renard had Hanna. I had to get her off his ship.

The ships manoeuvred alongside, taking care to offset their spars so their two sets of rigging wouldn't tangle. Renard's men threw lines across and our sailors secured them to the Fortuna. Our men threw the Fortuna's lines across to Renard's men. Hanna watched from their deck with a guard standing either side of her. When the ships were rafted together, gates were opened and the doctor and I stepped onto Renard's ship.

What would Henry say about my imagination if he could see me now? The motley group of men on deck had skin colours that ranged from light brown through yellow to black. There were no muscular giants although one tall man amongst them stood out. Hanna must have been taken below. The tall man stepped forward. The mist had cleared and the light from the rising sun glinted off a gold earring.

"Are you the doctor?"

Dr. Basset nodded. "I am. The boy is my assistant."

"If you save our captain's life, we'll return the girl."

"And what if, despite my best efforts, your captain dies?"

"You'll be sorry."

The doctor swallowed then said "Where is your captain?"

We were taken to a spacious cabin that ran the width of the stern. Doctor Basset bent over the man in the bunk.

"It's his hand," said the tall man who had followed us.

The doctor unwound a blood-stained bandage from the man's right hand, although hand was an exaggeration for the mess of mangled flesh and bone splinters that were radiating red streaks up the man's arm.

"When did this happen?" asked the doctor, turning pale.

"A few days ago."

"I can't save his arm. The hand should have come off when it was crushed."

"And if you take his arm off?"

"If he's strong and the poison hasn't too firm a hold, he might recover."

The captain had the same wild eyebrows and oddly-hooked nose as the tall man beside us. I guessed they were brothers.

"Then do whatever you can."

"Bring water and cloths," the doctor said to one of our guards. "And get him on the table."

The half-conscious captain groaned as his men lifted him out of bed, laid him on the table and tied him down. Dr. Basset held his patient's head up and poured something down his throat from a small bottle.

"That'll knock him out," he said. He opened his bag, laid out his instruments and tied a strip of cloth tightly around the captain's arm just below his armpit. He cut into the arm and shaped a flap of skin and flesh that was still attached down one side. He tied off the large blood vessels. Then he had me hold the captain's shoulder down with one hand and steady his elbow with the other while he sawed through the bone. I'll never forget the sound as scraps of bloody flesh splattered about.

The festering limb smelled unpleasant but every now and again I caught a whiff of The Red Dragon smell. What was the doctor's connection to these men? I tried to decide which of my many questions was most likely to receive an answer and finally plucked up the courage to ask one.

"Why are you following us?"

"Following you? You were the last person I expected to see in The Red Dragon. I thought I'd imagined you until I met you on the Fortuna."

"So why did you leave Redruth?"

"To get away from that thug, Jory."

Had Jory coerced the doctor into helping him?

"Why did you knock me out and tie me up?"

"For your own good. You've been poking your nose where it doesn't belong. I couldn't have you telling tales to Captain Spargo."

A final stroke of the saw freed the festering arm. The fingers twitched, as though they had lives of their own, and I dropped the arm on the floor.

Dr. Basset filed a couple of sharp splinters from the shoulder stump and smoothed the bone as best he could. By the time he'd finished, his hands were shaking. Perhaps that's why he wanted me to sew the flap of flesh over the stump.

"Don't worry," he said. "I'll talk you through it."

That was okay for him to say. He hadn't seen how my stitches puckered Hanna's flannel shawl and refused to line up like Emile's. But at least *my* hands were steady. Dr. Basset took another bottle of liquid from his bag and poured it over the ragged flesh. Then he told me to knot the end of a length of silk and thread it into the needle.

"All the knots must remain on the *out*side, so the stitches can be removed. Start here," he pointed, "and keep the needle in from the edge so the flesh doesn't tear. Hold it firmly now. That's it."

And that was my first lesson in sewing up bodies. The captain's bloody flesh was slippery. He shuddered as I pulled the second stitch through and the needle shot from my fingers.

"Careful," said the doctor.

"I've lost it."

"There!"

The needle was stuck in my shirt sleeve. I rethreaded it and continued my grisly task. I had to grip the slippery needle hard and my fingers began to ache. Thank goodness my patient wasn't conscious. I was aware of Dr. Basset watching me closely. He leaned towards me.

"I know you think badly of me," he said, in a low voice. I paused, then continued stitching. "But it was for a good cause."

"What cause?"

"Furthering medical science of course. How can we learn about the body if we don't know what it looks like?"

"That doesn't make it right. Taking bodies that don't belong to you."

"How else can we get them? Even with the new law, people don't like to donate their newly departed loved ones for dissection by medical students. They don't care about saving the lives of others."

I wondered whether Henry would have minded being cut up by a medical student as I tied the last knot.

"Not bad," said the doctor, checking to make sure I'd left a drainage hole as instructed. "Now we just have to hope he doesn't die from blood poisoning."

The captain's brother strode in as I washed the blood from my hands. He ordered one of our guards to dispose of the sawn-off arm, took a look at my needlework and grunted. I glanced through the cabin windows. The Fortuna was framed by weird purple-coloured clouds.

"Can the girl go back to our ship now, sir?" I asked.

"We're not done with the doctor yet."

I had to find out where they were keeping Hanna.

"Then could I have something to eat, sir?"

The captain's brother looked at one of our guards.

"Take him to eat," he ordered.

I tried to memorize the layout of the ship as I followed my guard. He was barefoot like me, and not much taller, but his arms were thick and all muscle. I might be able to get away from him if I took him by surprise but what would I do then? I'd hardly have chance to search the ship with the entire crew looking for me. My guard saw me looking at his right foot. The big toe stuck out at an angle from the rest of his toes.

"I broke it and it healed like that," he said. "Think your doctor can fix it?"

"Ask him."

"Only I can't get my boot on to go ashore."

"I have a spare right boot," I said. "It's a work boot with lots of room in the toes. It might fit you."

I couldn't interpret his answering grunt. He took me to the galley and ladled something from a giant pot. Then he rummaged for a spoon that might never have been washed and told me to sit. I stirred the contents of the bowl he clunked down in front of me and wished I'd thought of some other excuse to explore the ship. A greasy gravy clung to hard beans and even harder lumps of something that might once have been dried beef. I swallowed a spoonful as I looked around the galley. Everything was covered with a greasy film and rat droppings trailed across the floor. Although we were far from land, a couple of flies buzzed around my head and there wasn't a clean pot or utensil to be seen. Still, if the captain's constitution was strong enough to survive food cooked here, there was a good chance he would survive my stitching. I forced down as much of the stew as I could then the guard walked me back along a different corridor.

We came to an open doorway. My guard grabbed my shoulder, shoved me inside, and slammed the door. I was locked inside before I realized what was happening. There was nothing in the cabin except for the built-in bunk. I pulled on the door but wasn't surprised when it didn't give. I couldn't think what to do next. But I wouldn't learn anything useful locked inside. I banged on the door several times and called out that I needed to pee. No one came. The lump above my right ear ached. I lay down and tried to think up some kind of plan. Surprisingly, they hadn't searched me when I came aboard. I still had my knife tucked beneath my shirt but using it seemed like a quick way to end up dead.

Chapter 33

Would Hanna's kidnappers kill us if our patient died? I had to rescue Hanna before it came to that, but how? The gently rocking ship and stuffy cabin made it hard to stay awake. I paced the floor a few hundred times while I tried to come up with a plan. If I put one heel against the toe of my other foot I could take twelve steps before I had to turn. My innards struggled with the greasy stew. Maybe I'd think better lying down.

I woke to a rolling ship and recalled the purple sky I'd seen earlier. We were thumping against something. The Fortuna? The wind was blowing up something wicked. My cabin door rattled and my guard burst in.

"Come with me," he said.

"Where's Hanna?"

"None of your business."

We climbed stairs to the main deck. I couldn't go back to the Fortuna, not without Hanna. If only my head would stop aching. I took some deep breaths and wondered what on earth to do. If I could distract my guard, I could hide on their ship. Stow away. They wouldn't expect that. But then what?

The scene on deck had changed drastically since I'd come aboard. Men wrestled lines and hung off spars in their attempt to trim both ships while the wind whipped up everything that wasn't tied down. Plumes of spray shot across the decks as the two ships butted each other then strained apart.

"Bring me that boot," my guard yelled above the commotion. "And be quick about it or the girl will be sorry."

Men were busy untying the lines that held the two ships together as I hopped onto the Fortuna. Could I exchange the boot for Hanna? It was the only thing I had to bargain with. I bounced off posts and walls as I ran down to steerage, grabbed my old boot and ran back to the gate in the bulwark. As I reached it, one of Renard's men released the last of the Fortuna's lines and threw it back onto her deck. It landed at my feet and the two ships began to pitch apart.

"The boot," yelled my guard.

Behind him a figure crept across the deck of their ship. Hanna! I threw the boot high into the air above Hanna's captors who were busy securing lines. My guard, with eyes only for his precious boot, collided with them. One of them swore and they began to push and shove each other. While everyone was distracted, I grabbed the end of the line at my feet and yelled "Juuump." Hanna charged across the remaining width of deck and leapt towards the Fortuna. She almost made it but came down one stride short and plunged into the sea.

With the line now tied around my waist, I looked down. The last thing I wanted to do was jump into those foaming waves but if I didn't, how would we get Hanna back on board with our ship bucking like a wild horse? I held my nose and plunged, thinking this would be a stupid way to drown. The line jerked tight and Hanna's arms closed around my chest. My head went under then came up again. I coughed and tried to breathe. Hanna yelled "Relax." She was holding my head out of the water. I felt a great heave as we were hoisted clear of the waves. I seized the line with both hands as it dug into my waist. Hanna's arms tightened around me. Then other hands grabbed at us. They pulled us up through the gate and we slithered onto the rolling deck like giant fish.

"Bet you glad now I made you practice bowlines 'til you could tie them in your sleep."

Emile grinned down at me. He helped me untie the rope around my waist and by the time

I was sitting up, breathing normally again, Hanna had been whisked away.

"You best dry yourself," said Emile.

The wind plastered my sodden clothes to my body. I stumbled back to my bunk and struggled to undo buttons with shaking hands.

"Let me help," said Father, appearing out of the gloom.

We stripped off my wet things and he wrapped my towel around me, then folded me in his arms.

"Well done, Wyn," he said.

We stood like that, me shivering despite a sudden warmth inside, until Mac arrived with a steaming mug.

"Well done, laddie. I thought you could use a hot toddy."

Father let go of me and cleared his throat. I sat on my bunk and breathed in rum-laden fumes that cleared my head.

"How's Hanna?"

"Och, she'll be fine. She's a plucky lass. Now tuck yourself under your blanket and get warm."

The glow in my chest blossomed as I sipped Mac's toddy. The lump above my ear stopped throbbing. I snuggled beneath my blanket, relieved that things had worked out so well. Everything, that is, except my leaden lunch. I could track its progress by the churning of my innards.

Luckily for me, the squall was short lived and the wind was dropping by the time I made my way to the head. I felt much better after I'd got rid of the stew and went to find out what Mac knew of the day's events.

"Is Hanna really all right?" I asked him.

"As far as I know. Och, here she is. I'm afraid supper's a wee bit late."

"I'm glad I haven't missed it," I said. "The stew on the smugglers ship was revolting. And you should have seen their galley. Flies and grease and rat droppings everywhere!"

"No wonder they don't behave like rational people," said Mac, and we all laughed.

"The doctor said they were smugglers but what would they be smuggling?" I asked.

"Maybe opium into China. Or items with high taxes like silk and tea," said Mac. "The captain says there are still a few slave ships operating."

"I'm still trying to sort out what happened," I said. "How did they get you onto their ship, Hanna?"

"There were four of them in a row boat below me. With the mist I didn't even see them until they reached up and cut the ropes to the bosun's chair. One had his hand over my mouth so I couldn't call out and minutes later they were hoisting me onto their ship."

"But what were they doing there," asked Mac.

"I think they were looking for Dr. Basset," I said. I told them about Monsieur Renard with the chewed ear.

"So when they saw Hanna, dangling over their heads like a gift from heaven," said Mac, "they realized they could use her to get what they wanted."

"But did they only want Dr. Basset so he could treat their captain," I posed, "or were they after him for some other reason?"

"He cheated them," said Hanna.

"How?" asked Mac and I together.

"I don't know. I couldn't hear everything they said, but he owed them money and the man with the chewed ear was very angry. The captain's brother made him promise he wouldn't do anything until the doctor had finished treating their captain."

"He smoked opium." Mac stirred a large pot above the stove.

So that was the strange smell. Next thing I knew I was telling them about the body snatching and how the doctor had threatened to lock Father up in Bodmin Asylum. It felt good to finally tell someone.

"What did they do with the bodies?" asked Hanna.

"Sold them for medical students to practice on," I said. "At least, I think they sold them."

"Opium can be an expensive habit," said Mac.

A sudden thought occurred to me.

"Where's the smugglers' ship now?"

Mac and Hanna exchanged glances.

"Let's go and ask the captain," said Hanna.

"Don't you worry," said Mac. "The doctor can nae harm your father now."

The mate had sent the captain to his cabin for a rest and we found him there looking grey and tired.

"We lost sight of the other ship soon after we untied from her," he said, in answer to our question. "The doctor was still on board."

"About the doctor," Hanna began. And we told the captain about the body snatching and Monsieur Renard and what Hanna had overheard.

"I realized the doctor was smoking opium in his cabin," he said, when we'd finished, "but it was too late to turn back and put him ashore. I told him that if it interfered with the care he gave anyone aboard my ship I would see to it that he never worked aboard a ship again. Of course I had no idea he was such a scoundrel. That does explain why he didn't want to board the smugglers' ship though. Which reminds me, how exactly did *you* end up on their ship Hanna?"

Hanna and I exchanged glances and my face grew hot.

"It was my fault," I said.

"We found the bosun's chair on deck," said Hanna.

"And," I butted in, "Hanna was showing me how it worked."

"And the smugglers were out in a rowboat. I think they were planning to board our ship and find the doctor."

"But when they saw Hanna they took her hostage instead," I finished.

"I see," said the captain, who looked as though he didn't see at all. "Well, whether it was your fault or not, Irwyn, it was extremely brave of you to assist the doctor and then jump into the sea to save Hanna. I shall be eternally grateful."

"So will I," said Hanna. "I don't know how I'd have got back on board if you hadn't had that line tied to you. Not in that wind with the ship plunging about."

Her golden brown eyes sparkled and I longed to get her alone.

"Well, if that's all sir?"

"Yes, Irwyn, you may go. Hanna, sit down. I need to talk to you."

Over supper everyone was talking about the smugglers and Hanna's escape and what might happen to Dr. Basset. It had been a long day, despite my afternoon nap, and when I jerked awake for the second time, I excused myself.

I unbuttoned my shirt and sank onto my bunk only to feel a hard lump beneath the rumpled blanket. I lifted it back and found a small cloth sack. Inside, was a dagger and a wooden box. The dagger's handle was decorated with birds inlaid with something white and shiny that caught blues and greens in the lantern light. The box was carved with curved shapes that overlapped each other. I lifted the lid to find strange silver coins inside.

I stared at the coins for some moments before my tired brain told me they may well have been stolen. I looked around. Good. I was alone. I shoved the items back into the sack and thrust it beneath my blanket wondering what this meant. Had someone hidden the sack hoping to retrieve it later? I didn't normally go to bed this early. I knew I should take the sack to the captain but all I really wanted to do was sleep. I yawned. I'd take it in the morning. I unbuttoned my trousers, slid them off and lay beneath my blanket. I was nodding off for the third time that evening when a new thought woke me up again. What would the thief do if he came to retrieve the sack and found me in bed with it? Would I be in danger? Would he try to make me look like the thief? After all, it was common knowledge I'd been looking for ways to earn money. There was the captain's missing sextant too. I sighed, got out of bed, pulled on my clothes and grabbed the sack.

Chapter 34

Hoping the captain hadn't retired for the night, I was rushing along the hallway that led to his cabin when Pickersgill came barreling out of a doorway and barged into me. I dropped the sack.

"What have you got there?" asked Pickersgill.

"Nothing."

I bent to grab it but Pickersgill beat me to it. He pulled out the carved box and dagger and a sneer curled his upper lip.

"Looks like I've caught our thief," he said.

"I'm not a thief," I said, too loudly. "I found these. I'm taking them to the captain."

"Taking what to the captain," said Mr. Reddiman, coming to see what was going on.

"Irwyn has *found* some stolen goods," said Pickersgill.

People began to gather, my father among them.

"I *did* find them and I'm taking them to the captain."

I tried to grab them from Pickersgill but he snatched his hands away.

"*I'll* take them to the captain," said Mr. Reddiman, holding out his hands for the items.

"Then I'm coming with you," I said.

"Oh, he'll want to talk to you all right," said Mr. Reddiman, "but not tonight. He's a bit under the weather and he's gone to bed. We'll deal with you in the morning."

And by then Pickersgill would have had time to tell everyone I was the thief.

"I'm not a thief," I called to Mr. Reddiman's retreating back. Two of the miners gave me an odd look as they came out of the dining room.

"Come on," said Father. "We'd best go to bed." I followed him down the hallway. "Where did you find those things?" he asked.

"Someone hid them in my bunk."

"And you've no idea who or why?"

"No. And now everyone will think *I* stole them."

"But the captain thinks well of you. He wouldn't spend so much time showing you how he sail his ship if he didn't."

Father didn't know that the captain hadn't given me any lessons since the big storm that had blown us into the Devil's Triangle. I was afraid he was having second thoughts about me, although Hanna had said he was uncharacteristically tired and forgetful of late.

"Could you put in a good word for me with the captain tomorrow?"

"Of course, don't worry," he said. "I'm sure the truth will come out."

But I did worry. I opened my diary and jotted down my thoughts before the last man to bed blew out the lantern in the hope this would help me to sleep:

If the captain doesn't trust me he's unlikely to help me find work on a ship.

If the captain is unwell Mr. Reddiman might take charge in the morning.

How did Pickersgill know the box and dagger were stolen???

The morning would be Friday the thirteenth. I hoped that wasn't a bad omen.

When daylight gloom showed around the steerage door, I slipped out of bed and made my way to the captain's cabin. He was seated in front of his mirror in the middle of his morning shave.

"What brings you here so early in the day?" he asked, his chin half covered with foam.

Whether it was this, and his rumpled hair, I don't know but he looked as though he'd aged ten years since I first saw him fourteen weeks ago.

"I know this sounds unlikely, sir, but last night I found a sack hidden in my bunk."

The captain listened to what had happened and was about to speak when there was another knock at his door. It was Mr. Reddiman. He gave me an annoyed look and told the captain his version of events. The captain held up the wooden box and dagger.

"Can you tell me anything else about these, Irwyn? Have you any idea who hid them in your bunk or why?"

"No, sir."

"You haven't seen anyone hanging around in steerage who shouldn't be there? Or anyone acting oddly?"

"Not since the doctor."

"Hmmm. As far as we know, Dr. Basset is still aboard the smugglers' ship so we can hardly blame him for this. Thank you Irwyn. That will be all."

I left, hoping that his being "eternally grateful" included trusting me.

I heard nothing more of this matter and assumed the captain believed I'd told him the truth but on more than one occasion I looked up to find someone watching me. I was sure I was being kept an eye on. On top of this, we were only days away from Virgin Gorda and I still didn't know what I was going to do when we arrived. Then something else happened that upset me.

Chapter 35

Tiger's kittens had been roaming the ship for some time now and he, or rather she, had become her old elusive self. I was cleaning up the galley after supper one evening when I happened to glance in her crate. She was there, lying very still and when I touched her she didn't snarl or claw me. She didn't move at all. I told Mac and Hanna who said it was lucky her kittens were old enough to get by on their own. I lay awake on my bunk that night and it came to me that we should hold a service for Tiger. As soon as it was light, I got up, cut a strip from the end of my blanket with my knife and sewed it into a cat-sized bag. At least Tiger would have a decent burial.

I took the bag to the galley but Tiger's crate was empty.

"Where's Tiger?" I asked Mac.

"Och, Hanna took her last night."

I went to find Hanna.

"Where's Tiger?" I asked.

"Tiger's dead," she said, giving me an odd look.

"I know she's dead. I've sewed her a bag so we can give her a proper sea burial."

"Oh," said Hanna.

"Oh what?"

"Well ... I didn't know," she said. "I threw her into the sea last night."

"Just like that?"

"She was a cat. A bad-tempered cat who hated people."

"But she did her job. She kept the ship free of vermin. And she provided us with successors. That's probably what finished her off."

"She was starting to smell, Irwyn. Things go off quickly in this heat."

"If we threw everything that smelled overboard, there'd be nothing and no one left on this ship."

I stomped off. It was only some hours later I was able to admit that Hanna was right. Tiger had been a bad-tempered cat. Even so, we could have acknowledged her usefulness.

* * *

I reached the galley the next morning as Mac was leaving. He grabbed my arm.

"Come and see," he said.

"See what?"

He didn't answer until we were up on deck. Then he pointed. "There she is, the fat virgin. See her outline? There's her head."

The island's green hills swelled towards a brilliant sky. They did look like a fat woman lying down.

"That's why Columbus named her Virgin Gorda, the fat virgin."

We were there! My breath caught in my throat as my heart began to race. The island grew larger as we watched.

"I don't know what I'm going to do," I blurted out. "I'm terrified of working underground."

Mac looked surprised. "I'd no idea, laddie."

"Is there anything you're really afraid of?" I asked.

I didn't think Mac was going to answer because he just stood at the rail gazing at my new home but after a minute or two he said simply "Fire."

"Fire?"

"Fire on board a ship made of seasoned wood where the only place to go is the ocean. Sometimes I have nightmares about it."

"And yet you're a sailor?"

"The best way to handle fear is to face it. One of the greatest fire hazards on board ship is the galley stove. If I'm the cook, I have control over that."

But how could I have control over the mine?

* * *

Most of the passengers were on deck by the time the mate shouted orders to furl the sails until only three handkerchiefs were flying. He posted lookouts at the bow. Then the helmsman turned the ship to starboard and crept around a coral reef into a quiet bay. Pickersgill came past at the double on another of Mr. Reddiman's interminable errands, stumbled, and went sprawling. Hearing the thump and exclamation as he went down hard, all eyes turned on him. Out of his trouser pocket rolled two of the captain's intricately carved chess pieces. Pickersgill grabbed them, looked up, and saw it was too late to hide them.

"I found them," he blustered. "I was bringing them to you."

"Where did you find them," asked Mr. Reddiman.

Pickersgill hesitated a moment too long. Mr. Reddiman picked up the chess pieces, hauled Pickersgill to his feet and marched him off to see the captain. Later that day I was summoned too. Hoping I wasn't in trouble again, I knocked on the captain's door.

"I expect you'll be glad to get this back," said the captain.

He placed Mother's locket in my hands.

"Pickersgill?" I asked.

The captain nodded.

"He had quite a haul. He confessed to selling my sextant too. I've dismissed him. He'll have to find his own way home."

"Thank you." I hung the locket around my neck. "I'm glad you know it wasn't me, sir."

And Hanna wouldn't have Pickersgill hanging around on the voyage home. I should have felt relieved but it occurred to me that his wasn't the only kind of dishonesty.

"I still feel sorry for Pickersgill," Hanna said, after I'd apologised for my losing my temper over the way she'd thrown Tiger overboard. "He's struggled all his life. He only sold the sextant so he could buy some warm clothes. He said he was so cold."

"But he tried to make me look like the thief!"

"How?"

"He's the one who stopped me when I was taking the stolen items to the captain after he'd hidden them in my bunk. He let the boar out too."

"You don't know that."

"So he just happened to conveniently be watching when the boar was chasing everyone round the ship? For someone who normally made himself scarce it's rather a coincidence that he appeared whenever I was being blamed for something I hadn't done."

I still didn't know what to do about the mining company but I knew I had to tell Father about Henry. Our relationship seemed to have shifted over the course of the voyage. He'd told me he was proud of me on more than one occasion.

But he wouldn't be proud of me when I told him how I'd left Henry to drown in the mine.

Part Three
Virgin Gorda

Chapter 36

Monday July 16ᵀᴴ, 1838

We had to report to the mine on Wednesday. The day after tomorrow. Perhaps that was why I was finding it so hard to leave the small ship that had been my home for three and a half months. How had those months passed so quickly?

"I wish you were sailing home with us," Hanna said, during a goodbye made awkward by the fact that I wished for the very same thing.

"I will be next year." I gave her a quick hug and, when she'd gone, kicked myself for not stealing that kiss I wanted. Emile found me saying goodbye to the pigs and leaned his elbows on the half door. "Your daddy, he be lookin' for you. He can't wait to step ashore."

"That's hardly surprising. I doubt I'll ever get him aboard another ship," I said.

Emile smiled.

"Do you ever regret going to sea?"

"Nope. This a beautiful place but one small island and I want to see the world. If I stayed here I'd likely be cookin' and cleanin' and havin' children."

I looked at him and my puzzlement must have shown in my face because he laughed.

"Don't tell me Hanna won her bet?"

"What bet?"

He laughed again and I had to wait until he'd finished.

"We had a bet on how long it would take you to figure out my name is really Emilie."

"Emilie? but that's a ... you're a ..."

"Woman," said Emilie.

And now I wondered how I hadn't seen this before, with her small, neat hands and the way she'd looked after me.

"But you dress like a man."

"It's more practical. On the ship and ashore. A woman on her own gets hassled, 'specially in a sea port. No one takes any notice of me dressed as a man. I can pretty much go where I like."

"What about the other sailors on board?"

"I do my job, like the rest of them."

First Tiger, and now Emile. I didn't know what to say.

"I'll tell you somethin'," said Emilie. "In this life, you got to make your own luck 'cause it sure don't come lookin' for you."

"So Hanna bet that I wouldn't guess?"

"She said you couldn't see what was in front of your face."

Emilie left, still chuckling to herself.

The captain was on deck, bidding goodbye to the passengers. He still looked tired.

"Thank you for everything, sir" I said. "And don't forget your promise to come and get me next year. Emilie knows where to find me."

He smiled. "It's I who should be thanking you, Irwyn. Without your help, Hanna would still likely be on the smugglers' ship with Dr. Basset, wherever they are. I loooo ffff glllllllll."

He fell to the deck as unintelligible sounds came from his mouth. I stared in dismay. The left side of his face looked as if it had dropped somehow. I didn't know what to do. People began to gather and Mr. Reddiman quickly rounded up four crew members. They each grabbed a limb and carried the captain off to his cabin. I caught sight of Father.

"There you are Wyn, I've been looking for you."

I told him about the captain.

"Sounds like apoplexy," Father said. "Some people recover. Some don't. Emile's going to take us to his brother's house. Come on."

Not knowing what else to do, I grabbed my bundle of belongings and followed. All I could think of was that if Captain didn't recover, he wouldn't come back for me next year.

Rémy's house did indeed look out over the ocean that spread, turquoise blue, beneath us. It was a strange-looking house made from bits of old boats, packing crates and barrels that could all have been scavenged along the shoreline after high tide. The roof was thatched with leaves. The windows, hung with old sacks, were open spaces that allowed the island breezes to blow through.

"How do you close it up?" I asked Rémy, who looked a lot like his sister but taller. He laughed.

"No need," he said. "Anyone take anythin' it because he need it more than I do."

Rémy hugged Emilie, then showed us our rooms. I'd never had my own room before.

We'd barely settled in when someone came from the ship with a message. Rémy said he'd be back soon and he and Emilie hurried down the hill to the jetty. Father and I sat on the shady porch and I was wondering how to begin what I had to tell him when we saw a group of men climbing the hill. As they drew closer, I recognized sailors from the Fortuna who were carrying the captain. Hanna was with them and when she saw me she broke into a run.

"The captain's right arm and leg won't work," she said, close to tears. "He can't stand or sit or speak."

I didn't know what to say so I grabbed her hand.

"Rémy and Mr. Reddiman agreed that he can't stay on the ship in this state. Rémy said he must have lots of rest with good food and sunshine if he's to recover so we're going to stay here with you."

"But what about the Fortuna?"

"Mr. Reddiman will sail without us. We're to stay until the captain's well enough to travel back to England."

"Then things might still work out. If the captain's recovered when the Fortuna returns next year, he'll be able to take command of the ship again."

"Or he'll move in with Aunt Harriet. He told me after my capture by the smugglers that this voyage would be my last. I said he wouldn't send me to live with Aunt Harriet if he loved me. And now this has happened."

Fat tears rolled down her cheeks and, with everyone else gone inside, I pulled her into my arms. If the captain couldn't sail his ship, I'd be stuck here on Virgin Gorda, working the mine.

Chapter 37

Emilie was right about her brother's cooking. He fried up fish fillets that melted in our mouths while Father helped Hanna get the captain settled. Hanna was spooning fish broth into the captain's mouth when sailors delivered the rest of their belongings. Despite what Mac said, I'd decided I couldn't work down the mine but what if they wouldn't give me work above ground? I needed a plan and my brain had thrown out a half-formed idea. If only I could make it work. With Emilie's words about making my own luck fresh in my mind, I seized the chance to sound it out and walked back to the wooden jetty with the sailors.

"You forgot something?" they teased me.

"What's Mr. Reddiman like to work for?"

"Tough, but fair." said one.

"I'd rather be on his ship than a lot of others," said another.

We rowed out to the Fortuna. I was probably wasting my time. Mr. Reddiman had never liked me but I had to try.

The mate-turned-captain was studying charts in the captain's cabin.

"Yes?" he said, when I knocked on the open door. I couldn't read his expression.

"You're sailing the Fortuna back to England."

"I am."

"And Pickersgill's been dismissed."

"He has."

"Which leaves you short-handed."

"It does."

He wasn't the most talkative of people.

"Could I have Pickersgill's job?"

Mr. Reddiman stared at me. His frown wasn't encouraging.

"He told me it was his first voyage so I probably know as much about sailing as he does."

I crossed my fingers behind my back. "I really need this job. I promise I'll work hard. You won't be sorry."

"You almost cost me my job in Charlestown," he said.

"It won't happen again."

He sat without speaking while I silently chanted, please, please, please.

"The captain thinks well of you. So do Mac and Emilie. And you've proved to be willing and eager to learn ..." he paused. "So yes, the job is yours. Don't make me regret this."

"There's one more thing. Could you pay me now?"

Mr. Reddiman laughed. Not good.

"What's to stop you from jumping ship?"

"I swear to you I won't, and you know me well enough to believe me." As soon as the words were out I regretted the latter part of that sentence.

"What do you need the money for?"

"Because I don't want to work down the mine so I have to pay off the mining company for my passage."

Mr. Reddiman thought for a while longer.

"Tell you what," he said, "I'll give you half your pay now and you can have the other half like everyone else when we dock in London but you have to promise me two things. One that you won't tell anyone or else they'll all be wanting advances, and two that you'll earn your money because if things go wrong on this voyage my job will be on the line."

"I promise."

"Wait here."

A few minutes later he counted half my wages into my outstretched hands. "Be on board by 6 a.m. We sail on the afternoon tide."

Back on deck, I leaned against one of the pigpens and tried to sort out my thoughts. I could simply sneak away from Rémy's early next morning. People ran away to sea all the time. But that wouldn't be right. I had to try to explain to Father even though he probably wouldn't want to see me again, ever. And I still didn't have enough money to pay the mining company.

"Irwyn!"

Mac's Scottish brogue interrupted my thoughts.

"I'm glad I saw you laddie. I've something that might cheer Hanna up."

I followed Mac down to the galley where he handed me a kitten. "The other two are boys, but this one's a girl. If we keep her we'll be overrun with little Tigers. I thought Hanna might like her."

The kitten curled up on my lap, purring, while Mac poured mugs of tea. He handed me one, sat down and looked at me as though waiting for something.

"I've asked for Pickersgill's job."

Mac's face creased into a grin.

"But I have to sort things out with Father. I don't want him to think badly of me."

"I'm sure he doesn't."

"He will when he hears what I have to tell him. And I still don't have quite enough money to pay off mining company."

Mac looked thoughtful.

"You could sell me that locket around your neck."

I fingered its heart-shaped gold, warm from my body and the sun.

"It was my mother's. It's the only thing of hers I have."

"Then how about I make you a loan and keep the locket as security. When you've earned the money, you can pay me back and it will be yours again."

I hesitated, torn between the thought of leaving Virgin Gorda with a clear conscience and parting with something that was priceless. But then I'd have the other half of my wages when we reached England.

"How much would you lend me?"

Chapter 38

It grew dark early on the island. I dawdled back to Rémy's as I rehearsed what I might say to Father. His strangeness had gone, hopefully for good, but he'd be upset that I was giving up a good job at the mine. However Oliver Twist had done what he could to change his life. I didn't know how that was going to turn out and of course it was only a story but, after Mother died, Henry told me we have to do the best we can with what fate hands us. And Emilie made her own good luck. I wasn't going to get anywhere by drifting along, delaying decisions, and doing what was easiest. Then again, I'd promised Mother I'd look after Father and now I was about to leave him. Would he be happy here?

As I walked back up the hill, I could hear drums and Rémy was singing. Everyone was on the porch that ran along an entire side of the house. The captain was lying on a bed of cushions. Hanna, Father and Rémy all had small drums between their knees. They stopped playing when they saw me.

Hanna was thrilled with the kitten and began thinking up names. I told Father I needed to talk to him and we walked out of earshot of the porch as I tried to find a place to begin.

"The day Henry drowned ... he *had* come up from his shift."

"But we found him in a flooded hole."

"Because he'd gone back down to look for you."

"What?"

We were beyond the glow of the porch lamp so I couldn't see his expression but I pressed on.

"When he reached the surface, I told him you were still in the mine. He said we had to find you and went back down. I was supposed to go with him but I slipped and my hat fell off and it went dark and everything began to spin and ..."

I paused on a sob. Father didn't say anything.

"I called to Henry but he didn't answer and I couldn't see so I climbed back to the surface and when you came up with Mr. Gribble there were people everywhere and I couldn't tell you what a coward I was." I stopped to take a deep breath. "I left Henry in the mine alone. It was my fault he drowned."

"It wasn't your fault."

Had Father really said that?

"If I'd stayed with him I'd have been able to help him out of that hole."

"Then why didn't you?"

"Because I can't breathe underground. The taste of earth makes me choke. I was terrified I was going to fall from the ladders and I couldn't see and I didn't know where I was going."

"Then if you hadn't had the sense to go back to the surface, you'd likely have died too." Father pulled me into his arms.

"If anyone's to blame it's me. If I hadn't been so affected by your mother's death, the two of you wouldn't have had to look after me. Wouldn't have thought you had to rescue me. But I couldn't help that anymore than I could help being seasick or you could help the way you felt down the mine." He paused. "Henry wouldn't want us eating our hearts out over something we can't undo."

I brushed a shirtsleeve across my face as I replayed Father's words.

"Do you remember falling into that sink hole?" asked Father.

"What sink hole?"

Father drew in a shaky breath.

"We'd gone on a picnic. It was Henry's eighth birthday so you must have been three. You were running over a grassy hollow and the ground caved in beneath you. When I lifted you out your mouth was full of earth and you were choking. I turned you over on my knee and thumped you on the back until you coughed and spat it all out."

"I don't remember."

"Well, you were frightened. We thought it best forgotten."

Could I have somehow remembered this without knowing? Was this why I couldn't bear to be underground?

Father left one arm across my shoulders and turned as though about to guide me back to the house.

"There's more," I said.

I told Father about Henry's coffin, the body snatching, and how Dr. Basset had threatened to send Father to the asylum.

"Oh Wyn."

Father shook his head and sighed. And I knew then that I should have told him all this long ago. He would have understood. And now I *had* told him, the cold, heavy stone in the pit of my stomach was gone.

"So what are you going to do now?" asked Father.

The others had gone inside so we walked back towards the porch.

"I've taken Pickersgill's job. I'm going to sail back to England on the Fortuna. I want to be a sailor.

Father had an odd look on his face.

"What?" I asked.

"Your grandfather was a sailor."

"How come you never told me that before?"

"He was a drunkard. He left my mother to raise me and my brothers on her own. She always managed to find us something to eat but I didn't realize until later that she often went without. She was thirty-four when she dropped dead one night. She'd taken on extra work so she could help me buy new boots."

That explained a few things.

"I took up mining because I was good at it and I'd sworn I would support my …" His voice trailed off. We were both silent for a while.

"There's still the problem of the mining company," I said.

"I'm sorry Wyn. I've had plenty of time to think during the past weeks. I should never have signed you up without asking you first. What will you tell them?"

"That's the problem. I have to be onboard the Fortuna by 6 a.m. so I need you to give them this."

I emptied my pockets and money belt onto one of the porch chairs.

"Where did you get this?" Father stared, wide-eyed.

"I asked for an advance on my wages and, well, let's just say I came by it honestly. Tell them I'm sorry to leave them a man short but I wouldn't have been able to work down the mine anyway and this should cover their expenses."

"Then everything's taken care of," said Father.

"Not quite everything. It means leaving you here, on your own."

"Oh, I'm better now. It's lovely here and Rémy's made me welcome. The other miners are a friendly bunch, and Hanna and the captain will be around too, for a while at least. Do what you must to get on and let me know how things are going when you can."

"The captain said the Fortuna would be back next year so I'll see you then."

"I'll be here. I don't think I'll be going anywhere for a long time."

We hugged again then gathered up the money and went inside.

* * *

Hanna didn't take my news nearly as well.

"I thought I'd be here with you," she cried.

"I'm sorry Hanna. This is something I have to do."

"But you don't have to go now. She's not sailing until tomorrow."

"He doesn't want to be late," said Father. A smile hovered around the edges of his mouth.

"Give me a hand with my things?" I asked Hanna.

I would have liked a few days to see Father settled. I would have liked to explore the island with Hanna. But most of all, I wanted to be aboard the Fortuna when she sailed. I took one last look around the room that had been mine for a few hours. Hanna carried my jersey and diary, although they would easily have fitted into my small bundle, and we strolled out into the island night. The heat of the day had faded leaving a warm breeze that played over my face.

"How's the captain?" I asked. I'd been so busy worrying about my own problems that I hadn't given much thought to Hanna. I thought of her comment to Emilie, that I couldn't see what was in front of my eyes.

"It's hard to know when he can't say anything, but I think he's … confused."

The night throbbed with the chirrup of insects and a rhythmic thump of waves breaking along the shoreline.

"Rémy says he's seen other people like this," Hanna continued. "How much they recover varies from person to person."

We walked slowly. Even so, we were nearing the jetty and I tried to think of something to say that would make her feel better. I pulled Hanna off the side of the road and faced her. She smelled of honeysuckle. I pulled her towards me and gave her a quick, clumsy kiss on the lips. Then someone was coming along the road, humming, and we moved apart again.

"Don't go," said Hanna. "Stay on the island with me. Please."

I had to clear my throat before I could speak. "I have to make my own luck," I croaked. "This is my chance."

Hanna thrust my jersey, my diary and a piece of damp paper into my hands, turned and ran back the way we had come.

"I'm sorry Hanna," I called after her as she was swallowed up by the night. "I'll be back next year."

She didn't answer. I carefully tucked the piece of paper into my pocket. Later, on the Fortuna, I took it out and held it under a lantern. Hanna had written her aunt's address on it.

* * *

When the Fortuna sailed out of the bay the following afternoon, it wasn't me waving goodbye from the beach, as I had so often imagined, but Hanna and Father. They shrank in size as the Fortuna pulled away from land and a breeze puffed out her sails. It occurred to me that Pickersgill must still be somewhere on the island. Still, it was too late to worry about him now.

"All right Tremayne," called Mr. Reddiman, not unkindly. "Tidy these lines."

I turned away and set to work.

Glossary

apoplexy   A stroke.

barque   A sailing ship with three or more masts.

befuddled   Confused.

biscuit   Ship's biscuit, sea biscuit or hardtack was
                made from flour, water and salt. Baked
                hard and dry it would survive rough
                handling and temperature extremes, so
                was a staple aboard sailing ships. Like
                other food onboard ship, it often became
                infested with cockroaches and weevils.

bowsprit   A pole or spar projecting forward
                from the bow of a ship.

chronometer   A timepiece without a pendulum that
                could keep accurate time on a rolling
                ship. Without this it was almost impos-
                sible to calculate a ship's longitude.

constable | A policeman.

Cornish pasty | The Cornishman's sandwich: An envelope of pastry filled with meat and vegetables.

earwig | A creepy-crawly insect with a long slender body, antennae and forceps-shaped back end.

fathom | Six feet or 1.8288 metres.

fester | Inflamed and generating pus.

flummoxed | Confused

hold | The interior of a ship below deck. Cargo is carried here.

hove to | Brought the sailing ship to a standstill by setting the sails so they counteracted each other.

jersey | British word for sweater.

knacker | A person who buys worn-out domestic animals or their carcasses, usually for use as animal food or fertilizer.

knocker | A mythical creature in Cornish mining folklore. About two feet tall and grizzled, but not misshapen, they live beneath the ground. Here they wear tiny versions of standard miner's garb and commit random mischief, such as stealing miners' unattended tools and food.

oui — Yes.

piskies — The Cornish pixie: a fairy race with old wrinkled faces, red hair and dressed in green or brown.

Qi — Pronounced <u>chee</u>. The flow of energy in living beings.

rouge — Red.

schooner — A ship with two or more masts and fore and aft sails.

sextant — An instrument used at sea to measure the altitude of the sun or stars and calculate the ship's position.

sink hole — A depression or hole in the ground caused by the removal of soil, bedrock, or often both from beneath the surface by water or human activity.

sniggered — The British word for snickered.

splice   Join two pieces of rope by weaving together one end of each piece.

steerage   The cheapest accommodation on a passenger ship – usually between decks.

swamp   To fill with water.

treacle   The British equivalent of molasses.

wages   British word for salary.

About the Author

Born near Tolkien territory in Birmingham England in 1951, Frances came to Canada in 1973 on a year-long visit with her husband Keith and decided to stay. While bringing up her family, Frances made time for her other passions: writing and composing poetry and she received much recognition, including the Marg Gilkes Award in 1995 from the Calgary Writers Association.

In part because she was not keen on history at school, she felt there was a need to present history in an easy-to-read format written for young adults, publishing three books in this genre:

Norman Bethune: The Incredible Life and Tragic Death of a Revered Canadian Doctor. Canmore: Altitude Publishing, 2004.

Arctic Explorers: In Search of the Northwest Passage. Surrey: Heritage House Publishing Company Ltd., 2010.

Yip Sang and the First Chinese Canadians. Surrey: Heritage House Publishing Company Ltd., 2011.

Her children's book, *Aunt Maud's Mittens,* was published by Scholastic (2007)

Throughout the years, numerous poems of Frances' have been anthologized in works such as *Dear Tomato; And the Crowd Goes Wild; The Steampunk Shakespeare.*

She also had two essays published in *Engraved, an anthology of Canadian Stories of World War One* (2014).

And an essay published in *Brought to Light, More Stories of Forgotten Women* (2015)

* * *

Outside of her dedication to family and writing, Frances was keen on sport and outdoor adventure, and seized any opportunity to feel the warmth of the sun on her face. Weekends would find her canoeing the rivers of Alberta and British Columbia, hiking or skiing in Banff, Jasper, and Yoho national parks. (She was the first female to be awarded the Million Vertical Feet belt buckle in Jackson Hole.) She and Keith settled eventually in Golden, where she enjoyed skiing at Kicking Horse Mountain Resort and cross-country skiing and snowshoeing on Dawn Mountain. When at home, Frances loved gardening, reflecting her desire to nurture, as her family well appreciated.

Frances sailed extensively with her family on the west coast of Canada with longer trips to the Caribbean islands, along the Dalmatian Coast of Croatia, in Turkey, and in the Greek Islands. Frances also visited many places including Egypt, Ecuador, the Galapagos, Machu Picchu, New Zealand, Australia, Russia, Lithuania, Estonia, Latvia, Poland, Germany, Italy, Spain, France, Romania, Bulgaria, the Czech Republic, and in 2014 she travelled through Kenya, Tanzania, and Zimbabwe on Safari. Her last trip was a tour of China and Southeast Asia in 2015.

Frances and Keith shared a thirst for adventure and love of cultures, people, and history. On her travels Frances sought out local museums, art galleries, historical sites, and a good cup of tea. She was always ready with a pad and pen, taking notes, names and dates, perhaps seeking inspiration for her next story.

Frances lived courageously and passed away quietly on September 4, 2015 at the age of 64 years, beloved wife, mother, daughter, grandmother, sister, aunt, friend, poet, and author.

RIP Frances. Your writing lives on.

For more information, see www.franceshern.ca

9 781460 290477